Loogie

Peter Gillies

Loogie

A·B·C·

abceditions

enjoy life & love others
be you & have fun

A·B·C· EDITIONS ◆ FRANCE

Loogie
ISBN 978-2-9584200-7-9

to those who love

Loogie

In the beginning...

God was in a good mood and more than pleased. Earth was looking very fine indeed. Life's myriad facets – so tightly interwound, interwoven, interfused, interflowing – interacted in so many interesting ways. By golly, he was tickled pink. He had been so clever!

Of course, like any beginner, he hadn't succeeded overnight. Granted, he'd had no trouble with the initial phase, sweeping up a sufficient quantity of cosmic dust to form planets round a star and setting the system in motion. That was child's play for God. Physics he could handle. But once he set his sights on settling down, biology proved a good deal trickier than he'd imagined; the first few aeons, he'd racked up a discouraging tally of unavailing trial and error. His downfall every time? Entropy. It had stymied him at every turn. The simple rule of matter was this: unless you could figure a way to reverse entropic inertia, you couldn't get the organic flame to sustain itself.

No wonder, then, that it was more by fluke than by design that he'd managed it at all. God's own dark secret was that he had no idea how he'd pulled it off, nor even if it were correct to infer that he had done it himself. Waking up one day from a nap, he had found a tiny protocell at his feet. How it had got there – and still more how it had been sparked in the first place – he couldn't rightly say; but since he was God, he naturally assumed its genesis lay with him.

Bursting with a neophyte's pride, God lavished his freshly spawned protocell with unflagging attention and cajoling from that moment on – and the day its plucky progeny evolved into a batch of protozoa, he knew he was in business. However, doing the math, he quickly realised that life forms of a more complex nature would require a readily assimilable source of concentrated energy to keep them running. 'Food' took him ages to develop and refine. It called for mastering more chemistry than he cared to stomach, but thanks to photosynthesis and oxygen-farting cyanobacteria, God was finally able to set the stage for the development of large scale vegetation, the *sine qua non* for capturing and storing incoming energy from the sun round which his Work-In-Progress spun.

With the sky now the limit and God winging it, his logbook predictably recorded a litany of harrowing escapes: OXYGEN CRISIS; SNOWBALL EARTH; CAMBRIAN EXPLOSION; GREAT PERMIAN EXTINCTION. Thankfully, irreversible collapse was narrowly averted time and again. Indeed, given the reassuring tendency that catastrophes seemed to have to not only sort themselves out but to give rise on the whole to advantageous twists, it dawned on God that achieving excellence was as easy as combining a flawed approach with serendipitous experimentation and unfettered flying by the seat of his tush.

Why, take the slipshod way he'd set the solar system in motion in the first place: if he had foolishly used a compass to trace Earth's orbit, or a carpenter's square to set his planet's axial tilt at 0°, the magical seasons would have never existed. They were the unanticipated after-effect of pure dumb luck.

Once he got underway with the Triassic, things really picked up. This first full-scale experiment with complex life forms was nevertheless a rough draft. Having learned from his early protocell experiences that parenthood was onerous enough without the additional burden of upkeep and repairs, God was intent on refining the mechanism that kept equilibrium in motion indefinitely. His aim to generate a steady state of organic self-perpetuation and self-sustainment required a food supply that would be both self-regulating and self-renewing; the whole thing had to work like a charm, capturing calories from the sun and turning them into motion, all the while maintaining an intrinsically delicate balance. Motion meant critters galore. Understandably, God's dinosaur phase was merely a trial run, but he lived it to the hilt. Dreaming up the most outlandish reptiles he could think of, he populated the Earth with an internecine zoo of Monstersauruses and Terroraptors, and a good many ages passed while he happily tinkered with various ratios of carnivores to omnivores and herbivores.

Lest all-too-easy-fodder and free-for-all-feasts give any one species an edge over others to the detriment of the whole, God finessed as best he could the doling out of their inherent advantages and disadvantages in even proportion. Even so, a sort of biological precession kept creeping in. Doubtless it was the protean nature of Life itself that brought chance into the picture – for be they vegetative soloists or gymnastic gametes, his biotic broods were gleefully exploiting a loophole proffered by natural selection: to escape the carnage of the food chain, all a species had to do was perpetually update its coping strategies. It irked the Creator in Chief, but short of extirpating them all in one fell swoop with a top-down apocalypse, God had little choice but to put up with their evolutionary antics. As he was forced to ruefully admit, Creation seemed to have a congenital Will of Its Own that even he couldn't tame.

All the same, the dinosaurs had to go. God was sorry to snuff them out and cover up the mess with sedimentary substrata, but the beasts had served their purpose. Besides, he didn't think they'd make good pets for his own pet project, which he'd code-named ADAM.

Ah, Adam! The venture was a tall order and likely fraught with unforeseeable risks, but God was of a mind to replicate himself in the mirror of Life. He wanted to create a host of living, breathing beings who would look up to him and coo, *'Abba! Papa! We love You! You're God, the Summa of Perfection!'* That was how God saw himself and knew himself to be, but he wanted to see his Glory reflected in the eyes of another, a soul of his Soul, a chip off his Block, someone who would sing his praises and love him as he loved himself.

For if truth be told, as the sole conscious being in a cosmos without end that stretched beyond his ken, the infinitude of his solitude was more than God could bear.

In short, God was lonely.

II

ON THIS BEAUTIFUL FRESH MORNING, God woke to the inspiring sounds of birdsong and burbling springs.

'O, Eden, Garden of Delights… I so do love your tune!'

He'd strewn the Earth with many botanically-rich gardens, but Eden was God's favourite nursery safe haven. Nestled in a land that was bordered by desert, it was warmly suited to growing a profusion of tasty plants and fruitful trees, all irrigated by numerous brooks and streams that fed cool pools of water for animals to drink from before eventually flowing into a river that traversed the valley in meandering arcs.

Betaking himself for a stroll, God came to a small rise in the centre of the garden, where a tall date palm was standing at least a full shadow's length from any surrounding vegetation. Walking up the slight slope towards the foot of the tree, he spotted a sun-dried gem that had fallen among the few tufts of grass colonising the soil. He picked up the date and popped it in his mouth.

Adam… Adam…

God ruminated as he chewed the sweet flesh. He had a clear picture in his mind of how Adam should be, but he had learned from the past that he could save himself a headache or two if he put his ideas to the test beforehand with a proof-of-concept prototype. He was bound to discover a flaw or two that would need to be addressed.

'No time like the present for fooling around.'

Swallowing the date, God cleared his throat and hocked a loogie. It hit the ground and quivered in the dust.

Stooping down, he kneaded the wet mess between his fingers. Drawing in more dirt until the consistency changed from soft mud to firm clay, God shaped a body patterned on his own in every way. It came off remarkably well, no doubt because he was working off the cuff and not even trying for perfection.

'By golly, just look at you, Loogie. You're a handsome devil. But don't think for one minute, you epicene layabout, that I'm going to spend My time making more of your kind by mucking with spit'n'soil every day. Folks of your ilk are going to have to take care of that themselves. Just like all the other critters.'

With this in mind and an extra bit of mud, God worked up a tastefully proportioned penis and scrotum and stuck the genitals between Loogie's thighs, where they belonged. Stepping back to eye the result, God made a face. The picture of perfection an instant earlier was now risible beyond measure.

'Great heavens. This is grotesque. There is no other word for it, Loogie – that's a fleshy-sheathed snake you're sporting down there between your legs. And I have a Rule: No Snakes in the Garden of Delights.'

Staring at the unsightly crotch, God mulled things over. To admire himself in Adam's regard, he needed Adam to resemble his Maker as closely as possible – and the appendage of two gonads swinging from a pole was definitely *not* something he had derived from the flawless contours of his own sexless Beauty.

Grabbing a stick, God hastily extrapolated some rudimentary biological calculations in the dirt. All animate beings had to be able to reproduce themselves. It was a Cornerstone – a Bedrock-of-Life sort of thing, the Key to the whole Caboodle. But the outcomes were concordant: no matter which form it took, asexual reproduction was not a viable option for complex life forms; by inhibiting genetic diversity, it impeded adaptivity and propagated a precariously homogeneous population. Like it or not, God had no choice: his ADAM project required ova and sperm. There would have to be males and females.

What to do? The organically logical penis-into-vulva model for mammal reproduction was a marvellous system, tried and true; he wasn't likely to find better. Still, in all the mammalian species he'd developed, the genitalia were aesthetically hidden from sight – underneath the tail in females, between the hind legs in males. They came into play when needed but otherwise kept a low profile back there in the rear, where they ran little risk of being seen or, worse, mauled and gored by the raging hooves and horns of sure-footed, head-butting suitors.

Tackling the problem from the other end to see if he could find a solution there, he used his stick to sketch out a plan for the female Adam. Straightening up, he considered his design. Clearly, the mammary glands posed no serious problem. They were shapely and appealing; they could almost pass for prodigious pecs. As for the vulva, it was wonderfully discreet and attractive in its own right. Reaching for a handful of grass, God arranged it on his female Adam's pudendum.

'If need be, she can hide it under a bit of fur.'

Hopeful that fur might be the fix, God started adding pubic hair to Loogie's crotch. He quickly lost heart – the male groin would need a full beard to conceal its protuberance in toto.

High noon and high time for a nap. God decided he'd sleep on it.

'What a morning we've had, little fella. Tomorrow, I'll start over and make Adam from scratch. Don't know what I'm going to do with his penis, though. Such a silly looking thing, waving about like that. You've no idea how preposterous you look.'

God was just about to squash his prototype into goo when it occurred to him that he might as well rehearse the final step of infusing it with his spirit – that, after all, was the distinguishing feature of the ADAM project: the creation of a being whose soul imprint was derived from his own. Leaning forward, God brought his lips close and blew gently on the inanimate face.

It happened almost immediately. Loogie opened his eyes. He blinked.

'Well, hullo there, My good Loogie. How about that? You're alive. You can't stay that way, though: you're just a prototype. Sorry, but I have to squash you.'

God raised his fist to obliterate his creation.

'Screw you, Pops!'

Loogie spit in God's eye. Before God could bring down his mighty fist, Loogie made a dash for it and scampered to safety in the underbrush.

III

'CONFOUND IT!' God wiped the spittle from his face. 'Loogie! Come back here!'

God ran after him, but it was no use.

'Where in blazes did he go?'

God looked everywhere that afternoon. It was the damnedest thing. Whenever he'd wanted to track down a miscreant from the primate order, one of those fur-covered precursors to the ADAM project, he'd just shake a tree and they'd fall into his lap. This time, he shook all the trees in the garden and got nothing but a hail of figs and hard nuts for his trouble.

'LOOOO-GIE... Come out, come out, wherever you are...'

The hellion kept himself well and truly hidden.

'Fine, then,' shouted God into the gathering dusk. 'No stories for you round the campfire tonight! See if I care.'

God lit a campfire when the stars came out, hoping his prototype would be scared of the dark and come crawling back for comfort, but Loogie never showed his face. It was God's first vigil. Only when a thin red dawn glowed in the east did he accord himself a few hours of sleep. When he woke, the day was well underway. He'd overslept the birds' matinal recital.

Thinking about his misadventure, God concluded that Loogie must be impure. Whether by its nature or because it had been contaminated by he knew not what, the date, he decided, was the cause of the mishap.

'I should have rinsed My mouth,' he noted, finishing a copious breakfast of nutmeats and figs. 'I won't make that mistake with Adam.'

God went down to the nearest brook and cleaned his teeth. It was another beautiful day in paradise. To no one but himself, he made a sweeping declaration.

'Let this be a Day to Remember! Today, I Myself, GOD, will create the first man, ADAM – the spitting image of his Maker!'

Banishing any thought of dates from his mind, God paced around in circles for a bit, working up a mouthful of saliva. Then, when he had got a good gob, he scooped up a handful of dust and dribbled the spittle into the cup of his hands. Working the wet and dry together, God made his pug and proceeded to shape his archetypal man. Predictably, the result fell shy of the serendipitous grace he'd achieved with the prior day's prototype. Adam wasn't nearly as fetching. He was a little too contrived. A little too stodgy. God was dissatisfied. Hoping to rekindle some blessed fortuity, he pushed one eye slightly lower than the other; he bent the nose a little to one side; he added a bit more roundness to one of the buttocks. Nothing improved the overall impression. He was trying too hard.

'Bugger it. Arms; legs; head; torso. Stands upright. Conveys the general idea. No one would mistake him for Me, but he looks good enough. Besides, if I make him too handsome, it'll go to his head.'

He was about to awaken Adam from his inanimate state when he remembered the penis.

'Oh, hell – that eyesore!'

He'd forgotten all about it. He was back to square one, none the wiser for his trouble and in no mood to postpone his project any longer.

'Maybe if I minimise it; shrivel it up a bit.'

Aiming for a self-effacing, unobtrusive rig, God fashioned a pared-down set of male attributes, affixed penis and scrotum to Adam's crotch, and hid the dangly flesh as best he could beneath a pubic mane.

Stepping back for a look, he shook his head disparagingly.

'One thing you can be sure of, My boy: with a doohickey like that, you will never be a god. But don't let it bother you. You were never meant to be one. That's My prerogative.'

Adam now stood complete, motionless before his Maker and awaiting the Breath of Life. The moment had come.

Conscious that a momentous occasion should be ushered in as such with giddy excitement and oratorical originality, God paused for effect and tried to think of something germane to say. Unhappily, Adam was so unappealingly plain that nothing apposite came to mind.

God settled for a rite shorn of pomp. Sticking to the essentials, he leaned forward and blew into Adam's face.

The eyes opened, blinked, and struggled to focus.

'I NAME YOU ADAM.'

The new man's eyes blurred as he took stock of what he'd

just heard. Heeding a natural urge, he spoke.

'Bââââ-dumb.'

God shook his head.

'No. Without the b's. Like this: ˈadəm.'

'Ââââ-duhm.'

'Say it, ăd′ăm. *Ādām.*'

'Âhdum.'

'Close.'

Adam was slow, but preneuroned with standard phrasing. His eyes focused and he looked at God.

'What is Your Name?'

'My Name? My Name is…'

God was about to say *God*, but he knew that, onomastically speaking, God wasn't a name. He gave it a moment's thought. What would be a good name? A name with built-in submission and obedience. That was the ticket.

'Yah. Call Me Yah.'

'Ââh.'

'No, jɑː. Say it, yä. *Yah.*'

'Ÿâââh.'

'I know. The consonantal Y is tricky. We'll work on it. For now, call Me Abba.'

'Ahba.'

'Close. Come along. I'll show you round the garden…'

IV

LOOGIE WAS HAPPILY snacking on some of the succulent, chewy dates that had fallen to the ground under the palm tree. They were delicious. He'd found plenty of other good things to eat in the garden, but these were his favourite. He heard voices. Thinking it better to skedaddle out of sight, he snatched up a handful's worth of the fallen fruit and went to conceal himself behind the foliage of a nearby pomegranate shrub.

'Now, over here, Adam, you'll see I've put in a *citrus paradisi*. The juice is somewhat tart, but you'll find the taste is superbly delicate and refreshing. No, don't pick one. They're not ripe at the moment. You'll have to wait a few more months before you can eat them.'

'Oooh, what's that?' said Adam, pointing to a lofty tree's gently waving fronds.

Approaching the palm with Adam in tow, God gave the tree a long, hard look. There could be no doubt: its fruit was either prone to spoilage or had a mysterious, hidden power that had escaped him. He didn't want to court unwanted repercussions. He spoke with utmost solemnity.

'Adam, I want you to listen to Me very carefully. YOU MAY

FREELY EAT OF EVERY TREE IN THE GARDEN, BUT YOU MUST NOT EAT OF THIS TREE.'

'Why?'

'That is a good question, Adam. I am now going to tell you why.' Thinking fast, God extemporised a specious basis for his proscriptive injunction. 'You see, this tree is a duplicitous tree. This tree confers a knowledge of Good. However, this tree also confers a knowledge of *Evil.* If you ever eat the fruit of this tree, this Tree of Knowledge, YOU WILL SURELY DIE.'

'What's *die?*'

'To die is like being eaten,' said God – *but in this case,* he added in his thoughts, *means being hammered by My Fist if you ever disobey Me.* 'Would you like to be eaten?'

'I like eating. Maybe I'd like being eaten too,' replied Adam with innocent stupidity.

God rolled his eyes. The brightest star in the firmament his progeny was not.

Well hidden but privy to every glaringly sophistical word of God's edifying instruction, Loogie hissed scathingly. *'Knowledge of Good and Evil. Just listen to you, Pops. If anything, it's you, the Evil around here. You were going to bump me off!'*

'Come along,' said God, taking Adam's hand. 'It's back to the fig tree for now. Time for your nap. And remember what I told you. Never eat the fruit from that tree, lest you die. To die means your death, and you don't get to eat when you're dead. Besides, it doesn't even taste good. But don't you worry. You can eat of all the other trees in the garden. You will never go hungry for want of food. And for your snack this afternoon, you can have as many figs as you like. There are loads of them on the ground, and more besides ripening to perfection.'

As they walked off, Loogie spit out the stone from the last of his dates. Deciding he'd better keep an eye on what they were up to, he stole out from behind the pomegranate and set about tailing them at a distance.

V

GOD SAT IN THE SHADE of the fig tree, listening to Adam snore.

The lad had tuckered him out. He was doing his best with Adam, but it was hard going. A certain spark, he realised, was missing. While God reckoned he could depend on Adam to till the soil and feed himself, it wasn't likely the two of them were going to share any transcendental conversations. His archetypal man would be obedient and submissive and sing praises on cue, but it was unlikely he'd ever win a wreath of laurels for his wits. A species perpetuator, yes; but hardly a prize.

'Maybe I can breed some improvement into the ADAM project via his mate,' said God, plucking a fig from a low-hanging bough and sinking his teeth into the voluptuous flesh. 'The one with the womb. The womb-man. Or wo-man. The one who bears the new life. The source of life. Eve.'

Concealed in a thicket and keeping watch, Loogie regretted not having brought along more dates. The sight of God eating a fig had set his mouth watering.

God gave the matter some careful thought. To bind them together, the species required a common thread; for that, he'd need a lead-in from Adam. What could he do without? Not the appendix. It was a good-bacteria dispensary for the gut after illness. Not the pinky. Adam was challenged enough. Plucking a digit off his pentadactyl hands would mean he'd have to learn base 8; worse, he'd look cartoonish. The more God chewed it over, the more it seemed his archetype had nothing to spare.

Adam stirred in his sleep and rolled over. That's when God noticed the ribs. To build the protective thoracic cage, he'd employed thirteen pairs, and the last three rows weren't even fully fledged: connecting them to the sternum like the others would have resulted in too much rigidity, so he'd simply left them to float in place. He weighed the odds. It wasn't as if the adrenal and pancreas glands would be all that much more exposed if there were only twelve rows. Besides, the T13s were the runts of the rib defence. God chuckled to himself.

'No one will be any the wiser.'

Licking his fingers clean, he nipped a bit off each T13, leaving Adam's spinal stalk with two L1 stubs instead.

Loogie observed what came next with rapt attention. First, God gathered up some rich earth and placed the two spare ribs on top. Then he drooled down some spittle and kneaded it all smoothly together until he had a suitable quantity of mouldable clay.

While Adam slumbered in the shade, God set to work forming Eve's alluring curves, her elegant limbs and shapely hands, her graceful neck and mesmerizing face. Loogie was captivated. His penis started to swell as he watched God sculpt two hemispheric lumps of soft firm flesh with areolate nipples; his procreative organ stiffened further as God shaped the folds of the woman's labia majora; and when the Creator gave her vulval topography a pert clitoral nub as a finishing touch, Loogie was brought to his knees with his fingers wrapped round his fully-gorged phallus – throbbing and bobbing with jaunty little jerks, handsomely erect, and pointing the way to bliss.

Well hidden in the bushes, Loogie was undeniably taken with Eve's beauty; but Adam, having woken from his nap and laid eyes on Eve, was positively spellbound. His own appendage shot up in a jiffy. He hastily grabbed hold and began pumping his pole for all it was worth.

'What are you doing, Adam?' said God, looking over his shoulder. He noted his archetype's busy hand and frowned. 'Stop doing that, you fool. You're going to – '

A precocious jet of semen interrupted in reply. The creamy ejaculate fell straight to the ground and pearled in the dust.

'Oh, for crying out loud, you ninny! Now look what you've gone and done. You've wasted your seed.'

'Who's that?' said Adam, trying to milk his wilting erection for an extra spurt of fruition.

'This is Eve, you loon. And you're supposed to squirt your goods inside her, not all over the garden, for heaven's sake!'

'Eve is a *her*?'

'Yes, a her. She's your mate. Your better half, most likely.'

'But she doesn't look like me. You forgot – she needs one of these.'

Adam gave his shrinking penis a wave.

'Don't be silly. She has a vulva, not a penis. She's a woman.'

'A woo-man?'

'Absolutely. As you've already seen. But also because she has a womb – which is where your seed is supposed to go, you masturbatory nit. Like I told you. Inside her. Not to the four winds. Now be quiet. I need to bring her to life.'

Leaning forward, God blew gently upon Eve's lovely face. She opened her eyes and blinked.

'I NAME YOU EVE.'

Immediately, she took a step back.

'Uh, hullo? You're too close. Do I know you?'

God's eyes widened.

'I… I'm Yah,' he stammered. 'I just made you. I'm your God.'

'Right. Well, let's not rush things. Besides,' said Eve, casting a deprecatory glance at Yah's featureless crotch, 'compared to your friend there, you're not in full fig.'

VI

'WHO ON EARTH does she think she is, putting Me in my place like that? Me, her Maker! And Adam's hardly my friend. He's My servant. *Servant?* What am I saying? He's My slave! That's why I made him. To be My slave! To praise his Master! To love Me! With all his heart and soul!'

Nursing his gall, God restlessly paced the length of the garden. He'd left Adam and Eve to their own devices, buck naked and unchaperoned.

'Just you wait,' he seethed, venting his bile. 'You'll see, Eve. Oh, he'll do for stud service, when you yearn for a poke. And you can harness him for donkey work. But don't think he'll ever be more to you than a dependable provider. Try him for conversation. Yawnsville. Even better: try him for wooing and wowing. You'll find out then, lady-love. Poet he's not!'

Nettled by an unwelcome impression that Eve might have a mind of her own, God decided he was in need of a holiday. He'd take the morrow off. It had been a trying week. The highlands to the south were pristine and verdant; he was sure to find any number of spring-fed pools in which to soothe his soles.

'They'll hear from Me, though, if they finish the figs.'

VII

ADAM WAS SHOWING EVE round the garden.

'Now, over here, we have a… a…'

The name escaped him, but the clusters of fruit reminded him of something.

'A what?' pressed Eve. Her tour guide had been annoyingly slow all morning.

'A… *grape*-fruit tree,' said Adam. With a didactic flourish, he treated her to an authoritative presentation. 'The juice is superbly tart, as you'll find, even if the taste is somewhat delicate and refreshing. You can't pick any, though. They're not ready. They have to be overripe before you can eat one.'

'And what's that?'

He followed her gaze.

'Oh, *that*,' said Adam, averting his eyes. 'No, you mustn't look at that tree, Eve.'

'I mustn't look at it?'

'It's better if you don't. Yah has said we must never, ever, ever, never eat the fruit of that tree. It's never ripe. It'll give you a tummy ache.'

Eve was intrigued. She set off for a closer look.

'Wait, Eve!' Catching up, he took hold of her arm and pulled her back. 'Not a good idea. We're not supposed to eat it. We're not even supposed to touch it. God said so.'

Eve jerked her arm free from his grasp. Adam's patriarchal ways were an ongoing affront. He'd been lording it over her since dawn. She didn't like it one bit.

'Why? What happens?'

'If we touch it,' said Adam, *'we –'*

'We what?'

He puffed himself up with pontifical conviction.

' – we die!'

The word meant nothing to Eve.

'I'm sorry, is that a problem?'

'Are you kidding? Of course it's a problem, Eve: it means we can't eat!'

'What are you talking about? What does *die* even mean?'

'Oh, you wouldn't understand. You're just a woo-man.'

Eve stared at him. Yah couldn't be serious. This was his idea of a mate? Heaven help her.

VIII

HIS THOUGHTS CARESSED by the sonorous yelps of jackals howling at the moon, Loogie had spent the better part of the night thinking about Eve. She was the most beautiful woman he could imagine. He was loath to admit it, but on that score, God had done good.

Warming himself by the early morning sun, Loogie looked out over the Garden of Delights from the vantage of a rocky outcropping at its edge. He could see the date palm in the middle of the garden and, further on, to the north, the leafy fig tree where he'd last seen Eve and Adam as the sun was getting low. Spying on them as they returned from a tour of the garden, he'd overheard Adam boasting to Eve about his ejaculatory prowess; but when they reached the tree, she'd refused to mate with him.

'No.'

'What do you mean, no?'

'It's a word. It's the opposite of Yah. Get it?'

'No.'

'Good. Now you understand.'

'But I need to, Eve. Look. It's sticking out like a horn. We can't leave it like that. Think of what might happen.'

'You're right. You might gore a goat. Or a sheep.'

An unnatural thought crossed Adam's mind. Eve interrupted his distracted reverie.

'Leave them out of it. You don't need them, and you definitely don't need me.'

'Yes I do. Yah said I was supposed to put my seed inside you,' insisted Adam, stepping forward. 'He said it, so you have to let me do it.'

'Back off. I'm not interested.'

'But why not? Yah made you for me. I want you. See? Don't you want me?'

Eve hesitated. She didn't want any physically intimate contact with Adam, but should wild animals roam into the garden at night in search of easy prey, she did want to have him near at hand: while he fended off fangs – or fed them, as the case might be – she'd have time to escape or climb a tree.

'It's not that, Adam,' she temporised. 'It's just that it's been a long day. I'm tired. My head hurts. Maybe I got too much sun. Let me sleep on it. I might feel better tomorrow, after a good night's rest.'

Adam was hurting too – his testicles were aching for release – but he reluctantly acquiesced to Eve's continence. Feigning a sudden cooling of his ardour, he pointed out that the woodpile wouldn't see them through the night.

'We're running low. I'll go get my hands on some firewood.'

Loogie laughed aloud, recalling the look in Adam's eye as he'd come charging into the undergrowth.

'Firewood! His stiffy would've ignited if he'd been stroking it any faster. I'm lucky he didn't catch sight of me. I could see it in his eyes: horse, sheep, goat, dog – he'd have jumped anything that turned tail.'

Loogie climbed down from the rocky outcropping and set off to rustle up some breakfast. He was in the mood for dates and he knew where to find them.

IX

When Adam returned later, Eve could see he'd be leaving her in peace. He was scratching his butt, and his penis drooped with indifference. Once the sun set, the chilly night air brought them both to the campfire, round which they shared a desultory conversation. Soon, Adam was yawning and ready for bed. That she later betook herself to lie down beside him for warmth was only because the fire eventually died for want of wood. He'd apparently failed to find more.

Adam was still sound asleep when Eve woke the following morning and decided to brave a walk by herself in the garden. An hour later, she was in the vicinity of Adam's grapefruit tree, a stone's throw from the tree he had warned her about. Drawn to it by curiosity, she stepped into the small clearing and was astonished to see a man sitting cross-legged beneath the palm – a man who not only was not Adam, but one who had collected for himself a small pile of the forbidden fruit.

Loogie noticed Eve as soon as she stepped into the clearing. He waited for her to come closer. Eve was on her guard but, inexplicably, felt sure she had nothing to fear.

'Hullo. Would you like one of these?'

He held out a plump, sun-ripened date.

'I'm not supposed to eat that fruit,' said Eve warily.

'Says who?'

'Says Yah.'

'Oh. That's too bad.'

Loogie pulled the date apart and freed the stone before slipping the date into his mouth. He savoured its fleshy sweetness while he tried his nonchalant best to peripherally eyeball Eve's enticing beauty.

'Has Yah really said you don't get to eat from every tree in the garden?'

'That's what Adam told me.'

Loogie raised his eyebrows but said nothing. He swallowed the date.

'We were here yesterday, you see, and Adam told me Yah has said we must never eat the fruit of this tree. We can eat the fruit from all the other trees in the garden, just not this one here in the middle. God says that if we eat it or touch it, we'll die.'

Loogie shrugged. He picked up another date and bit into it.

'Nonsense. Don't believe it. You're welcome to sit down, if

you like. Make yourself comfortable. I've been eating this fruit since day one. Look at me. Do I look dead?'

Eve had been looking at Loogie and admiring what she saw, but she appreciated the invitation to look at him with still more attention. He was beautifully sculpted and had a natural grace. The sight of him made her tummy flutter in a way that was new to her.

'To be honest, I don't know what die or dead looks like, but Adam seemed to think it was pretty bad.'

'Well, he doesn't know what he's talking about.'

That, curiously enough, tallied with Eve's impression. She kneeled, folding her legs to place her feet beneath her buttocks. She was suddenly self-conscious. She detected a faintly slippery sensation within the slit of her crotch. She liked it.

'You surely will not die,' said Loogie. 'Yah's just pulling the palm fronds over your eyes. He knows that the day you partake of this tree's fruit, your eyes will be opened and you'll be like him. You'll know Good and Evil.'

Eve's head was spinning from the sound of Loogie's dreamy voice.

'What's *Evil*?'

Loogie picked up a date and held it out to her.

'Why don't you find out? Decide for yourself.'

X

THEY WERE DELICIOUS. Eve was delighted. He was charming. She couldn't wait to see him again. He'd been so nice. And generous. Not only had he happily shared the fruit with her, he'd even suggested she could take some to Adam.

'You never know. It might open his eyes, too.'

Eve didn't know if it was the forbidden fruit or maybe something else, but she knew she felt completely different. In a good way. She felt alert and alive and full of desire for more of what she'd tasted – and she wasn't just hungering for that honeyed, fleshy, dark-amber-skinned fruit. She desired his company. His eyes looking at her. The sound of his voice.

When she got back to the fig tree, Adam was pouty.

'Where have *you* been?'

'You'll never guess. I met someone.'

Adam started.

'What do you mean, you met someone? There's nobody else here to meet.'

'Yes there is. I don't know his name – I didn't think to ask – but he's very nice and very smart. Here, look. He gave me some fruit.' She held out a date. 'Try one.'

Adam took the date and considered it. He hadn't seen one of these before. It looked like an oversized raisin.

'Is it good?'

'Why don't you taste it? Decide for yourself.'

Adam bit into the date.

'What do you think?'

His expression softened.

'Oh, that's good,' he said, salivating and smacking his lips as he masticated the toothsome morsel. 'Oh, yes. Very good. That might be the best fruit in the whole garden.'

'That's what I think, too. Now, what would you say, Adam, if I told you… that this is… *the forbidden fruit.*'

Adam stopped in mid-chew. His eyes opened wide.

'Don't think you're going to die, whatever that is,' said Eve, content to see that the fruit was having the desired effect. 'I've eaten a dozen of these already and I feel just fine. There's nothing wrong with this fruit. It's delicious. And I'm sure it's good for us.'

Striving to quell a mounting dread, Adam swallowed the mash of date.

'Now you've done it,' he said hoarsely. 'Now we know Good and Evil.'

'Right. Apparently, that makes us like God. We know Good and Evil,' said Eve. 'Me? I can live with it.'

Adam was petrified. Awaiting he knew not what, he quailed at the thought of what Yah would do. There'd be a hailstorm of wrath. *I'm dead! When God discovers that I know Good and Evil, He'll know I broke His Law. He won't let me eat any more!*

Recoiling from Eve's kind offer of another date, Adam proceeded to gorge himself instead on what he was sure would be his last meal of figs as he tried his level best to access this newfound knowledge that now apparently filled his cranial cavity to the brim. He'd swallowed the key to unlocking the riddle; his abdomen was churning and turning it; yet to Adam's consternation, he was stymied at every turn: the G'n'E intelligence remained locked away in the stronghold of his skull. Unable to crack the enigma, Adam was baffled to deduce that his brain, seamlessly hermetic, wasn't as easy to pick as his nose…

For her part, Eve was thinking ahead to the chilly night.

'What if I dream of snuggling up with my mystery man for warmth, only to wake and find myself entwined with Adam?'

The mere thought gave her the willies. Looking about, she realised there was no shortage of sturdy fig leaves. It kept her busy all afternoon, but by the time Adam had coaxed the campfire to life that evening, she'd sewn scores of leaves together to make fig-leaf ponchos for the both of them.

'What's it for?' asked Adam uncomprehendingly when she held it up for him to admire.

'To keep you warm.'

'But we've got the fire.'

'At night, silly, when the fire dies down. When we're sound asleep. Try it on.'

She showed him how to pass it over his head.

'I look ridiculous,' he complained, holding out his arms. He was the very picture of a sandwich-board crier for patchwork garden compost.

'But you feel warmer, right? That's what it's for. To keep you warm. But wait. Don't wear it near the fire. The leaves might catch. Here, take it off.'

Doing her best to make the evening a friendly one, Eve chattered on and on about anything and everything, save for what was really on her mind. Adam, however, quiet and withdrawn, only half listened.

*

Adam slept fitfully that night. He kept waking up, spooked by every ache, every pain. He still had no idea what Good and Evil were and it terrified him. His stomach was in knots.

'Why did I swallow that fruit?' he moaned, looking up at the stars. 'Why didn't I spit it out? That's what I should have done. But it was so delicious. It tasted so good. So good…'

With leaf-crushing suddenness, Adam sat bolt upright. The pyramidal pins of his understanding had aligned.

'That's it!' he exclaimed, smacking a fist into the palm of his hand. *'That fruit is good. And good is Evil!'*

In Adam's angst-addled mind, it made perfect sense.

'If something is good, you want to eat more; but because you eat more, you eat too much – too much of a Good Thing – and you wind up with a tummy ache. And a tummy ache is evil. The more perfectly Good something is, the more perfectly Evil the tummy ache it's sure to give you – and then you die! That's why God forbade us to eat of that tree's fruit; it's too Good for us. And everything that is *too* too Good is most *evilly* evil Evil.'

Eating just one had already left him ill with foreboding.

'Knowledge! Who needs it? Spare me ever learning more. I was better off before, when I knew nothing at all...'

Adam lay down and adjusted his fig-leaf pyjamas. Although relieved to have cracked the conundrum, he was dreading the upshot when Yah's all-seeing Eye would surely discern they'd disobeyed. Who knew what retributions they'd reap?

This was all Eve's fault. He'd be sure to point that out to her. She was wrong about the fruit. Still, he had to admit... she was right about one thing. The poncho kept him warmer.

XI

GOD WAS SINGING A LITTLE DITTY as he ambled through the garden, dappled by the rays of the early morning sun.

'A man will leave his father, a man will leave his mother... a man will join his mate and their flesh will make another...'

His month-long jaunt to the south had tickled his trotters and refreshed his spirit. He'd found the loveliest little east-west running valley – temperate to a T, it boasted a cascading spring, pools of cool, rejuvenating blue waters, and background music from the birds and the bees morning till night. Decidedly, the highlands suited him. Pretty as a picture and self-contained, the dell was a realm unto itself. Why, God had so enjoyed himself that he had christened it with a felicitously-coined acronym for *Highly-enchanting-and-very-enviable-nook.* Only a throne was lacking to make it fit for a king.

Still, much as his avidity for Eden had waned, it was good to be back. His old stomping grounds! He wondered how Adam and Eve were getting along. He chuckled to himself.

'I'll bet those two lovebirds are cooing and cuddling under the boughs, chirping sweet nothings into each other's ears.'

Hoping to observe them undetected before he announced his return, he began tiptoeing through the undergrowth as he approached the fig tree. He had come nearly within sight of the camp when a persistent rustling caught his ear. God glimpsed a mound of leaves walking on two legs. It was headed in the direction of Adam and Eve's water supply, a small, nearby brook.

'What in the world is that?'

No sooner did he spot the deciduous intruder than it disappeared out of sight among the bushes. God followed. There was no sign of the mutant leafage when he reached the brook. Snooping about, he found traces of its footprints along the bank. God bent down and gave them a careful look.

'Where are you?' he called, straightening up. 'I know it's you, Adam. Stop hiding. Come out, come out, wherever you are…'

God scanned the shrubs with an eagle eye. Although he was otherwise well camouflaged, Adam's feet were by no means countershaded and they gave him away.

'Ha! Olly, olly, oxen free!'

Adam sheepishly emerged. He offered an explanation.

'I heard Your Voice in the garden, and I was afraid.'

'Afraid?' God was truly surprised. 'Of Me? But why on earth so? And while we're at it, why are you covered with leaves?'

Adam blushed.

'It's because I was naked. Eve made this for me. To keep me warm at night when the fire goes cold.'

It struck God that the leafy garment was a stroke of genius.

'I see. Well, I can't say it's not an improvement. Very good. And besides that, what have you been up to? How's the garden treating you? Are you and Eve finding plenty to eat?'

Adam shifted uneasily from one foot to the other and said nothing. But his conscience was uneasy – and all at once, the floodgates burst.

'The woman!' blurted Adam. 'The one You gave me – it's all her fault! She gave me from the tree, the one with knowledge of Good and Evil.' Beating his breast, Adam confessed his heinous crime to the leaf-crushing tune of his *mea culpa*: 'I ATE! I LIKED! I SWALLOWED!' Driven to his knees by an urgent need to grovel, he threw himself prostrate on the ground.

God was dismayed. He didn't know which was worse, that Adam had transgressed his Law or that he was tearing his tunic to shreds. If the fool ruined Eve's handiwork, he'd expose himself anew.

'What are you doing? Get up! Don't make things worse. You've done enough damage as it is. Where's Eve? Damned if she hadn't better see to this quickly. And damned if she hasn't got some explaining to do.'

XII

ADAM'S RUSTLING LEAVES and God's huffing and puffing were a dead giveaway; Eve heard the two of them coming long before they reached the camp. Stretched out under the fig tree and still wearing her own leafy garb, she'd been enjoying the peace and quiet of a lie-in and fondling herself as she tried to think of a ruse she could use to give Adam the slip for the day. She sat up and gave her wet finger a pensive lick.

Moments later, Adam and God tramped into the clearing.

'Good morning!' she called in a cheery voice, not especially happy to see either of them.

Leading the way, God made a beeline for the fig tree. As he passed the campfire ring, he noticed several date stones lying in the dust. Eve watched him with innocent eyes as he strode up and came to a stop, his nostrils flaring. Only then did he see the small pile of forbidden fruit on the ground beside her.

He indicated the dates.

'What's this you've done, Eve? Adam tells Me you gave him this fruit to eat. And that you've been eating it, too. I told him it was forbidden. Didn't he tell you that?'

'He did. But I ignored what you said.'

God couldn't believe his ears. The nerve! She knew, and yet she'd flouted his inviolable injunction. He was her Maker, confound it. She had to obey him. It… it… well, it wasn't written anywhere in stone – yet – but, by golly, he'd see to that.

'I'm your God. So what I say goes. Why did you eat it, if you knew I'd forbidden it?'

'Why? Because of the other one. He told me that he'd eaten the fruit and that it was good. And that it made us like you.'

'The other one? What are you talking about?'

'You know. The one who's like Adam. He's here in the garden, too.'

'– the Snake!'

'The snake? Surely serpent's a nicer word. But he's no snake. He's a man, like Adam. Only better, actually. Anyway, he suggested I should try it. Seems perfectly fine to me, to be honest. I mean, it's delicious. And this knowing Good and Evil, and…'

Her voice trailed off. Standing to one side, Adam, wide-eyed with trepidation, was meaningfully shaking his head.

God's eyes, however, narrowed. What was this? She found Loogie better than Adam? She preferred a miscreant on the lam to his own hand-picked man? The hussy! There was no doubt about it: the dates had spoiled Eve's soul. She was a bad apple. His whole plan was on the brink of collapse. How dare she – against his Word! Did it mean nothing, that he was her God, that he could smite her out of hand in a righteous fit of fury?

'For now, fix the fig leaves,' he commanded, pointing to Adam's tattered attire. 'And stay put. I'll be back in a minute.'

ത

God betook himself to the far side of the clearing. This was Loogie's fault. He'd forgotten about Loogie. It was he who had meddled, the evildoer, contaminating his two archetypes with the root source of rebellion. It didn't augur well. What to do? He was of a mind to do away with the three of them, then and there – kapow! A laudable impulse. But unrealistic. He'd have to catch Loogie first. And besides, starting over was no guarantee things would go any better; if it weren't one thing, it'd be another. He'd learned that from the dinosaurs. This was the situation. He had best deal with it.

On the bright side, Adam was shamefaced and repentant. That would pay dividends: from now on, the schmuck would toe the line. He'd be a model of devotion and duty, a megaphone of love and praise for his Maker. On the dark side, Adam and Eve were both palpably incapable of resisting temptation. More troubling still, Eve was both audacious and wiful. To nip that in the bud, he'd have to be firm. If he backed down now, they might infer they were free to do as they pleased; which, of course, they were; but that was the last thing he wanted them to know. If they discovered they were free, they might leave him in the lurch – back where he'd started, in the infinitude of solitude.

Thankfully, they were young and malleable. There was still time. A firm hand now would shape them for life. They needed to be saddled, not just with guilt, but with consequences, too…

A curse! That's what he needed – a good curse or two. Eyeing Adam and Eve, he sniggered with malicious satisfaction.

Now in what way could he bedevil them without jeopardising his creation? Things had become such a convoluted jumble that even the most well-intentioned monkeying with Life's intricate workings could have disastrous repercussions; no, at this stage in the game, his only safe bet for one-upmanship was to 'afflict' them with woes that were already part and parcel of their condition but of which they were still ignorant; that way, they'd think their waywardness had earned them a demotion they would have been otherwise spared, had they but heeded his Word.

God fished around for some curses that were already destined to hound them.

'Old age? That won't scare them; they think they'll be young forever. Taxes? They'll turn tithe evasion into a sport. Death? It's too far down the trail. At their age, they couldn't care less...'

Then God had an epiphany. For Adam, a curse from which he'd never have rest – the daily grind! Up to his knees in weeds, foraging and farming, chores and sores galore!

'Ha! The grain-eater will never get over that one. By golly, he'll rue the day he ever crossed Me.'

And for Eve? What could he saddle her with? Mending and mopping? Rearing and raising? That was everyone's lot, Adam included. Moreover, in view of her crime, drudgery was hardly condign. God wanted something that would assuage his spite.

It hit him like a thunderbolt: what goes in with pleasure will come out with pain. That'd settle the score! God knew it was a cheap shot – to liken a woman's throes in childbirth to a curse was to draw a veil over the boon it bestowed on the foetus, that tranquillizing dose of endorphins supplied to the newborn through the umbilical cord – but he was miffed she'd found Loogie beguiling.

God moseyed back to where the unsuspecting targets of his spleen were cooling their heels in the shade of the fig tree. Adam was picking his nose and eating boogers. For her part, Eve was putting the finishing touch on her chances for another peaceful night. She held up Adam's fig-leaf poncho against the sun to inspect her repairs.

Then God arrived. He cast a shadow on her work.

XIII

'ALL RIGHT, YOU TWO – listen carefully. Brazenly flouting My orders, you have eaten from the tree that confers knowledge of Good and Evil. That was a bad move. You're not going to get away with it. You will be punished for your temerity. I will now tell you both what you're going to reap.'

Reaching up, he picked a fig for himself. He pulled it apart and checked for worms.

'Adam,' proclaimed God, taking a bite of fig and cursing with his mouth full, 'this one's for you. You have listened to your helpmate's voice, and so eaten from the tree about which I commanded you, saying, You shall not eat of it. Because of this, here is what I say: The ground is cursed for your sake. You will eat from it with much labour all the days of your life. It will yield thorns and thistles to you, and you will eat herbage from the field. By the sweat of your brow, you will eat bread until you return to the ground, from where you were taken. For dust you are, and to dust you shall return.'

Adam looked at the ground. *Dust! Talk about being cut down to size…* He shot Eve a scowl.

Turning to Adam's temptress with relish, God went on.

'As for you, Eve, by cavorting with that reptilian trickster, you have exposed yourself to his snaky guile: he has inveigled you into thinking it smart to be wise by dangling a dialectically tempting knowledge of Good and Evil before your eyes. For letting yourself be so easily deceived into writing off My Word forbidding that fruit, here is what you reap: I will greatly multiply your woes in childbirth. In pain will you bear children.'

Adam brightened a little – at least he wasn't the only one who was going to suffer – but Eve shrugged.

Surprised by her silence, God took another bite of fig.

'Maybe you didn't hear. It's a nasty one. In pain will you bear children,' he repeated, expecting to get a rise out of her.

Eve still said nothing.

Peeved, God sharpened his tongue. With no sound basis whatsoever, he added a spurious curse off the top of his head.

'More, your desire will be for the man I gave you, and he will rule over you!'

Eve jumped to her feet.

'What? Whoa there, Yah! Where on earth do you get this bunk? I'm not going to be ruled over by anyone. Not him, not you… not even that handsome serpent!'

But God was on a roll and in no mood to brook dissent.

'That Snake is accursed!' he vociferated, stuffing the last of the fig into his mouth. 'I say, because of what he has done, he is cursed above every other beast of the field. He will crawl on his belly and eat dust all the days of his snaky life, and between his offspring and your offspring there will be nothing but hostility. He will bruise your heel, and you will bruise his head!'

Eve rolled her eyes. *He's nuts. Obsessed. He's got to be jealous. I bet he envies snakes their all-knowing ways with small holes…*

Fully cognisant of Eve's overt disdain, God's blood began to boil. In a fit of pique, he dealt them an expatriating broadside.

'I've had it to here with your cheek! The two of you deserve nothing less than banishment. Both of you! Pack up your bedrolls by sundown. You are hereby banished from Eden!'

Storming off to the edge of the clearing, God turned round to append his verbalized seal – 'I have spoken!' – and then plunged into the undergrowth, leaving them shell-shocked.

Adam knew who to blame for this bombshell.

'You and your fruit! See what you've done? No more food!'

True to his Word, God made a grandiose show of hounding them out of the garden before the sun set that evening. To Eve and Adam's surprise, though, they discovered that Yah's bark was worse than his bite: his bombastically touted banishment from Eden cast them no further than a pistachio tree on the other side of the brook. Apart from finding their access to figs and fig leaves curtailed – obliging Eve to replace their fragile foliar outfits with more durable garments made of wool – their life in many ways continued as before in the months that followed. Not only did they enjoy the run of the garden as a whole for food, but – and this, to Eve's relief – they saw less of Yah.

Yet God was not absent altogether. Banking on future returns, he was keen to safeguard his investment by ensuring no harm came to his ADAM project's seed bank. To this end, he hatched a pure figment of his imagination: an air division of anthropoid sentries, specially fitted out with four-faces and four-wings apiece for duly monitoring all quadrants while keeping a wing out for cardinal points, plus head-to-foot plumage to improve aerodynamic performance. He was about to assemble a female division earmarked for breeding fresh recruits when he opted instead for open-ended sempiternity. *All it takes is one turning out like Eve to spell trouble... why risk it?*

Charging his avian minions to watch over his fledgling lovebirds like hawks, he posted them on the fig-tree side of the brook and cleared away some shrubs to afford them an unobstructed view of the pistachio tree; and to keep everyone on their toes and entertained while conducting their surveillance mission, he gave them a flaming sword to play with. They never seemed to tire of tossing it back and forth to each other and spinning it round and round in show-stopping circles.

Adam was impressed by the skilful sword handling, but Eve lodged a complaint the next time Yah checked in on them.

'Honestly, one of these days they're going to drop that thing and start a fire. Why garrison your cherubic garden gnomes in Eden, of all places? Can't you move them out to the desert?'

He could never say from where the idea for his brilliant riposte came, but seizing his chance to float an entirely fictitious yet perennial myth, God deftly launched an unsinkable hope.

'I'll tell you why, Eve. My cherubic gnomes, as you call them – though we can shorten that to cherubim – are here to guard the way to a tree I've not yet revealed to anyone: *the Tree of Life.* It's here in the garden, but well hidden, so that you'll never find it. For knowing you two,' he slyly declared, sowing a calculated subterfuge, 'no sooner would you see it than you would stretch out your hands, and take, and eat... AND LIVE FOREVER!'

Eternal Life. Ha! It was a master stroke. Reconcile themselves they might to knowing Good and Evil, but never to having been debarred from everlasting life. Even if they wandered far from the fold, no sooner would their mortal lives draw to a close than fear of impending death would drive them back into his arms. Like prodigal sheep, they'd regret their disobedience; bleating repentance, they'd promise their love; lavishing him with adoration and praise, they'd plead for a deathless reprieve, imagining he held the Secret somewhere in his garden.

Thanks to this whopper, God was sanguine...

They'll worship Me forever.

XIV

NOT LONG AFTER, God gave Adam a pep talk. Reminding the whelp of his procreant duties, he instructed him to beget sons and daughters who would be God-fearing and compliant.

'Get on with it. It's time you consummated things. I didn't make you young and healthy just to till soil. And stop spending so much time with the goats. They can look after themselves.'

Try as he might, though, Adam found himself with a dearth of opportunities to access Eve's wellspring of life. What's more, every morning his mate drew up a daily list of chores that kept him toiling from sunrise to sunset in their ever-expanding farmstead comprising fields and orchards, pastures and pens. Adam concluded that in her book, his role amounted to husbandry from start to finish, with the foreseeable result that he was so tuckered out by the end of the day that God's exhortation – *Get it on and multiply!* – fell by the wayside.

That was exactly how Eve wanted things, for in blatant disregard of God's over-the-top curse, her desire was in no wise for Adam. She longed for her mystery man.

The only trouble was, she had no idea where to find him. Most every day, Eve went out of her way to check on the grapefruit… taking a circuitous route to the citrus so that she could casually pass by the palm. For a while, the clearing round the tree was strewn with date stones, but apart from that, there was no sign of Loogie. Later on, though, and much to Eve's chagrin, the dates that fell to the ground and dried in the sun went uneaten, except for the ones she collected herself.

ꕥ

Spring warmed to summer. The eagle-eyed cherubim continued to report that the two lovebirds had still not engaged in their expected mating courtship. Worried that Adam may have been lulled into dancing zoophallic polkas with the goats, God went to check on his ADAM project's point man. Why wasn't he following protocol?

'Are You kidding? Eve doesn't let me near her, not even with my eyes: despite the summer heat, she continues to keep herself well concealed. She lets me strip down naked when I work in the fields, where she doesn't see me anyway, but she dresses me down if I don't I cover up my crotch with this itchy thing whenever I'm around her. Can You beat that?'

In God's view, the woollen loincloth that Eve had concocted for her mate was a tasteful solution for shielding the ungainly sight of Adam's pendulous organ, but he said nothing.

'Whenever I see her, she's always clothed, and at night she insists on wearing pyjamas. But frankly, it makes no difference, because at the end of a full day of chores, I'm bushed. Once the sun's gone down, climbing into bed appeals to me more than climbing on top of Eve. And You want me to mate with her? Fat chance. Tired as I am, I'd snore before I'd score.'

God considered this. His Earth-system's equilibrium required that each species' sustenance be, contradictorily, both plentiful and scarce. If food were too easily obtained for a given species, the result would be an exponential increase in the size of its population; by sheer force of numbers, they would overwhelm the practical limits and upset the natural order. On the other hand, if food were hard to come by, or if the quantity were insufficient when the breeding and nurturing seasons rolled round, the species would find itself first worn down and then losing ground; if nothing intervened to reverse the trend, extinction would loom, pure and simple.

With few natural predators chasing their defenceless hides, humans had a clear advantage over most other species with regard to the system's checks and balances. For this reason, God had favoured making the getting of food and the raising of their young a full time occupation, lest humans breed like rabbits and overrun the globe. But if they were too tired to breed at all, the whole purpose behind creating them in the first place would be nixed in the bud.

Clearly, he'd miscalculated somewhere – how or when, who could say? One needn't look for a scapegoat. *Errare divinum est.* What mattered in the here and now was making the necessary adjustments to meet his objectives.

He decided to cut Adam some slack.

'Tell you what: we'll make it a rule. Six days will you labour and do all your work. Come the seventh, you get to lie around in bed as much as you like. A whole day off to rest up and ready yourself for *procreativa penetratio*. How does that sound?'

Adam liked the idea, all the more so when God assured him that he'd see to increasing crop yields to cover the one-day shortfall: 'I WILL CALL FOR THE GRAIN, TO MULTIPLY IT, AND I WILL MULTIPLY THE FRUIT OF THE TREE, AND THE INCREASE OF THE FIELD.' But he didn't see how it would make Eve more receptive.

'Well, you never know,' said God. 'Maybe she's no less tired than you. But mark My Word, Adam: I'm only making tomorrow a day of rest so you can put your willy to work.'

ග

Leaving nothing to chance, God upped the next night's thermostat to HEAT WAVE, and so drove Eve to imprudently shed her self-protective modesty: realising she was simply too hot to fall asleep, she sought relief by pulling off her pyjamas.

In the middle of the night, sensual dreams took hold of her. Writhing naked under the stars, moaning softly, she imagined herself luxuriating in Loogie's embrace as, spooning her from behind, he sailed the virile vessel of his manhood up between the recumbent pillars of her thighs… pushed his procreative mast into the slippery folds of her sex… and reached a crescendo with a deep, forceful thrust that made her gasp aloud – *'oh! YES!'* – as the glans kissed the eye to her innermost chamber.

However, Eve was just as suddenly disappointed: her dream lover stopped abruptly and withdrew. Even so, she woke with a smile on her face. She slipped a hand between her legs and sighed contentedly. Her vulva was unusually wet.

All at once, she was startled by the distinct impression that Adam was on his knees near by, crawling back to his bed. Eve spun round and sat bolt upright. Peering into the darkness of the no man's land that lay between their separate sleeping areas, she could just make out a curled-up lump frozen to the spot, an abject incubus hoping to escape detection.

'Adam! Was that you?'

For wordless reply, he farted.

XV

'BUT WHERE HAVE YOU BEEN all this time?'

'Well, I started by going that way,' – Loogie pointed west – 'and I came back from that way,' – he pointed east – 'and from there' – west – 'to there,' – east – 'I went every which way.'

He traced a circle in the air.

'I missed you.' Eve was playing with his dark curly strands. 'I wish you'd asked me to go along.'

They were lying side by side in the sun, on a grass-covered knoll. The rumble of a distant waterfall lent an enchanting air. Loogie had brought some dates. He offered one to Eve.

'How about you? What have you been doing?'

Eve related what had happened since he'd left. Her pregnancy. The birth of her and Adam's son. Their homesteading routines in rhythm with the seasons. Loogie's fingers wandered in quiet arcs of sensual exploration as she spoke. He delighted in her eyes, her expressive face. Her voice was more lovely than birdsong. She was beauty incarnate.

'I'll have to be getting back soon,' sighed Eve. 'Cain will be waking up from his nap. He'll start crying, if he's hungry.'

Loogie cupped his hand round her breast and gave it a gentle squeeze. Milk started to trickle from the nipple. Pulling her close, he took the teat in his mouth and began to suckle.

At first – steering clear of the cherubim's wider circle of surveillance and keeping an ear cocked lest God should happen by – Loogie had continued residing in the garden so that he could catch occasional glimpses of Eve. After a while, though, he'd grown restless. Eden was all well and good; but live there forever? It wasn't long before he'd filled a homemade satchel with dates and set off to explore. His odyssey took him clear round a nearly landlocked sea and taught him that paradise was overrated. So long as his days were free from want and terror, he found that he could be happy most anywhere. In the course of his travels, he discovered the charms of the windswept desert; the heart-stopping thrill of leaping from seaside cliffs; the challenge of crossing high mountain cols between snow-laden peaks; and the breath-taking scenery of alpine meadows carpeted with colourful spring flowers.

Having left the cocoon of Eden behind, Loogie made the Earth his home and pillow. All the same, his longing for Eve never waned. No matter how far he strayed, the compass needle of his desire still pointed to her.

Eventually, his feet turned him round and brought him full circle. She'd found him that morning waiting for her under the date palm when she least expected it.

They kissed. Eve rolled on to her back and pulled 'the Snake' on top of her. Wrapping her legs round his waist, holding him tight, she abandoned herself to being carnally possessed by the man she loved, passionately fulfilling their mutual desire.

ɞ

Yet it had been by Adam – goaded into the breach by God – that she'd had her first child.

Galled by the whole affair, she'd named the boy Cain to mark her displeasure with the way Adam had acquired his access and driven home his pike without her consent. In Eve's view, it spoke volumes about the sort of man he was. Still, she had a child to raise now, and she counted on the boy's father to work from dawn until dusk to provide for their needs.

'That'll teach him,' she reasoned. 'He who pokes, pays.'

But some weeks after her and Loogie's happy reunion, when she knew for certain that her deepest longing had been fulfilled, she conjectured Adam would cry foul.

'He's probably like God – a jealous type, with a bent for patriarchal rule. He might try to bring me to heel with a leash.'

Eve was anxious to confer with her lover, but he was keeping a low profile. There was no telling when they might tryst again;

on account of Yah's vigilant watchers, Loogie only sought her out when he was satisfied the coast was clear. Still, she had to know: when *their* love came to *her* push, would he pick up and carry *his* share of the load? And what about Cain? Though her feelings for the boy were decidedly mixed, even unmotherly, she still felt the tot should be old enough to fend for himself before she moved on. And then there was the question of where they might go – whenever they'd discussed travelling as a family, Loogie's promising ideas, she noticed, were soothingly long on hypotheticals but unsettlingly short on fundamentals. Sure, he adored her and made wonderful love, but was he up to taking his tribe on the road? Nomadic life didn't scare her; it even sounded fun; to feed three mouths a day, though, and in due course maybe more, they'd need to top up rovers' luck with the hard-won yields of earthbound hard work. Would Loogie pull his weight? Or was he all come and go?

It was dicey. The more she thought about it, the more Eve realised she held the best cards. It had been four weeks at most. She'd only had one child; Cain alone as precedent didn't make an ironclad rule; besides, Adam was no wiz when it came to maths. Eve shrewdly decided to hedge her bets. If she took the initiative now, he'd never suspect he'd been taken for a ride.

XVI

'IT IS A LOVELY garden.'

She stood at the edge of a rocky outcropping, admiring the paradise spread out below. Her companion picked up a small rock and threw it, aiming for a palm tree he saw in the distance. The stony projectile fell short.

'I could think otherwise, no doubt, but I'm sure my lovely queen Asherah would tell me I'm wrong.'

'Are you saying it's *not* a lovely garden?'

'I'll grant that it's a lovely garden… seen from our vantage here. But does this garden foster delight? That we don't know. More to the point, has he managed after all this time to kindle the spark of Love? We've been waiting for ages.'

She turned to her one true love and smiled.

'So?'

He loved it when she smiled like that. Her wiles always had their way with him.

Asherah mischievously took his hand and placed it upon the gibbous orb of her breast; its swelling nipple kissed his palm.

'What do you mean, *So?*' he countered, closing his eyes and drawing a breath. 'Without love, no garden is complete…'

His voice trailed off. Having taken his hand away from her breast, she was now moving it in circular strokes on her belly, arousing his wildest desire.

In truth, it never left him. Having floated for eternity in tenebrous, timeless separation, their first-ever touch had sparked an impassioned explosion of cosmological delight so breathtakingly luminous that in the nano-instant that followed – for the sheer fun of it, insouciant of where it might lead or what it might entail – they had unbridled their universe. Exponentially stoking its unbounded fractal branching with their intimacies, they had been swirling ever since in an endlessly evolving love dance in the space spawned by the kaleidoscopic magic of their two conjoined souls… and despite their binary arc in time having dawned countless aeons upon aeons ago, yet his desire for his dialectical compeer abided undimmed, his love a never-sated yearning, an infinitely recommenced reaching for his polar counterpart. He could no more resist than wish to escape.

'Why do you do this to me, Ash?'

Asherah's smile softened.

'But 'El, you know why…'

Guided by her firm grasp, his hand came to rest where she wanted it most.

'It's because I love you.'

She shepherded his fingertips to her divine source of life.

'Always.'

XVII

LOOGIE HEARD SOMEONE afoot in the greenery, approaching with an assured step.

Scooping up a few fallen dates, he retreated to the edge of the clearing and quickly hid himself behind the pomegranate's leaves. *It's surely Yah making a round*, he thought.

But then he heard voices.

'… me wrong, Ash. I'm not saying he's inept. I'm just saying he's peculiar. He dragged out that dinosaur phase ad nauseam, after already taking forever to get his planet up and running in the first place.'

Loogie's eyes widened with surprise as he observed a tall woman emerge from the bushes on the other side, followed by a man – at least, it seemed like they were woman and man, only their beauty was breathtaking. They appeared luminous, even other-worldly.

'I know, 'El. Honestly, if we hadn't stepped in when we did, I don't think he'd have ever managed. Do you?'

'Frankly, it's to wonder.'

'Though I did so hope he'd pull it off on his own, despite his being so much slower than all the others.'

Loogie was entranced. Eve was delightful; but this woman? *She's divine! What I wouldn't give to know her.* Yet no sooner did he consider her companion than he realised that he found him to be every bit as appealing. It gave Loogie pause. He had never felt the slightest attraction to Adam; but to this man? Here was a new feeling…

'I'm not sure slower is the word. More like static. Look at his siblings. All light aeons ahead of him. Even our youngest. It's creating an imbalance.'

'Well, we might get lucky,' said Asherah. 'Surely by now he's succeeded in making a likeness, don't you think?'

She approached the palm and sat down, leaning back against a smooth part of the trunk. She spread her legs a bit and began fondling her vulva.

'If he has, it would be a miracle,' said 'El, sitting down beside her and following her example as his penis stiffened and rose, his spark rekindled by the sight of his queen.

Crouching in the shadows, Loogie watched the two beings as they casually pleasured themselves, side by side. His own hands couldn't help but imitate theirs. Feasting his eyes on the couple under the date palm, he found himself suddenly pining for possibilities hitherto unimagined. He didn't dare give himself away, but he couldn't help wishing he could join them… though he was at a loss to know to which temptation he'd want to surrender first – the glistening cleft, or the glorious staff.

A tiny moan escaped Asherah's lips as she turned to kiss 'El's shoulder; sliding a hand across his thigh, she took hold of his erection and gave it a subtle tug to signify that she wanted him. Without a word, her companion rose to his feet and stood himself before her, placing his raised hands on the trunk of the tree for support as he leaned forward with an easy grace. All the while continuing to pet herself with one hand, Asherah grasped her lover's phallus with the other and started caressing the tip's smooth, taut skin with her tongue, pushing gently at the meatus as she moistened the glans with her saliva. Then she opened her mouth wide and drew him in.

They coupled that way for a short spell to the melodious air of the palm fronds above being rustled by a passing zephyr, before 'El pulled his penis free of Asherah's buccal love-port and kneeled down to kiss her, their tongues meeting and tasting and teasing each other as he combed his hands through her long wavy mane, his fingers tightening round handfuls of tresses and holding them tight as she played with his curls and tweaked his lobes. Presently, 'El's attentions led him lower. Pausing along the way to briefly nibble at her neck, he then left a meandering trail of wetness as his tongue navigated down past her collarbone to the realm of her breasts, where his teeth closed round a nipple with an amatory bite. Asherah bent her head and tickled her face in his tangly locks while he lovingly suckled her teats, each in turn. Giving him a gentle nudge with her forehead, she turned his attention still lower, where her fingers had gone to splay her swollen labia seeping with desire. 'El needed no further prompting. Laying himself prone before his queen, he slid forward between her legs and began licking his consort's beauty, his tongue exploring her vulva's outer folds and probing its intimate depths while his hands went in search of her belly; there, his fingertips set to work, tracing love trails across the smooth skin, stoking the fire within. Asherah closed her eyes, her smile the quintessence of truly carnal bliss.

Spying on the lovers, Loogie was achingly torn between the unparalleled allurement of 'El's divine buttocks, rhythmically rising and falling of their own accord as he indulged his cunnilingual pleasure, and Asherah's sublime breasts, cradled and kneaded in her palms as she pinched their pert nipples – and so rivetingly prurient was his heady, peeping-Tom complicity that Loogie, forgetting himself entirely, heaved a groaning sigh of burgeoning desire.

Asherah opened her eyes.

Catching sight of a figure amongst the shadows at the edge of the clearing, her smile widened.

The miracle had occurred.

XVIII

EVE HAD NEVER LIKED the weekly day of rest: it had emboldened Adam to think it conferred upon him certain rights, and it was tiresome to have to fend him off a full day running. Today, though, it would serve her purpose. She decided she'd surprise Adam with some coquettish charm. He was gullible enough, she knew, to fall for it. And although she wasn't much one for exhibitionism, she realised that, if she played her cards right, she could dupe two cads with one trick: so long as she staged an eye-catching show, the watchers would be sure to deliver a full write-up to Yah. He'd be just as thrilled as Adam. The pervert.

'Hey! You there!'

At the sound of Eve's voice, the cherubim on the other side of the brook stopped their swordplay.

'Be useful for a change. I'm going to see Adam about something. Cain's asleep here in the manger. If he wakes up, cross over and look after him until I get back.'

The cherubim were disconcerted. Was she joking? God hadn't said anything about babysitting. They waved the sword menacingly, but Eve wasn't waiting for a reply. She turned on her heel and left them speechless – not only because they were at a loss for words, but because God, distrusting them not to caterwaul or screech or hoot at all hours in the garden, had forbidden them to speak when not in his presence or within the strict confines of their encampment. It was his metaphorical way of keeping them caged.

Leaving the sword-twirlers to hold down the fort, Eve made her way to the meadow where Adam was pasturing the goats and sheep. Day of rest or no, the animals had to graze. As she reached the field, she passed a pair of cherubim who were lazing about, counting sheep and looking bored to the bone, no doubt anxious for sundown.

'Adam?'

Caught unawares, he looked up with a guilty petulance. Eve saw that he was plaiting strands of hemp to make a cord.

'Are the goats keeping you busy?' she asked, somewhat waggishly. She jestingly prodded his thigh with her foot.

'The sheep need watching, too.' He set the unfinished cord aside and reached for his loincloth. 'Besides,' he added sulkily, 'it's not like I've got anything better to do on my day off.'

'Why are you putting that on? Don't feel you have to on my account. I know you like to be naked out here. It's perfectly fine by me.'

This was news to him. He gave her a blank look.

Poor thing, thought Eve. It's true she would hate to be in his soles, routinely spurned by a woman he so desperately longed to bed. He just couldn't appreciate how unappealing she found him. Why, in his worst moments, Adam embodied every unappealable reason a woman could possibly have to swear off sex – such that just envisioning what she was on the verge of putting herself up to do made her dizzy with aversion. Still, it wasn't as if the alternative were better. Both Adam and Yah were unpredictable; it was safer to circumvent their suspicions than risk reaping their ire. She had a clear intent and a woman's means to achieve it. Besides, what the two never knew wouldn't hurt them. Deciding she may as well make the best of it, she gave the two cherubim a friendly wave.

'Aren't the goats and sheep pretty?' she said. 'I wonder what it's like to be a goat…'

Eve walked a little way off, though not too far. Adam was now watching her with heightened curiosity. A nanny goat bleated and approached to investigate Eve's outstretched hand. She looked back at Adam. Fixing him with an impish eye, she unfastened her shoulder strap and let fall her spun-wool shift.

Adam's eyes nearly popped out of his head.

It was then that Eve took the plunge. Turning round to face the cherubim, dropping to the ground on all fours and arching her back, she pointed her butt squarely in Adam's direction. If he knew anything about animal husbandry, she reckoned, he'd know what he could do with it.

And the best part of all? While he went in for his thrill, she wouldn't have him in her face.

XIX

'YOU'RE SURE? And he put it in the right orifice?'

God hardly trusted Adam. He most certainly did not trust Eve. The cherubim's latest report had come as a surprise, to say the least.

'We're sure. And we know he got a good look, up close, before he mounted her.'

'He didn't spill his seed before entry?'

The cherubim vigorously shook their four-faced heads. Yah, looking up at them from where he sat in a pool of soothing blue waters, had duly noted the conspicuous mastheads the telling of their tale had given rise to. They squirmed self-consciously.

'All right, My winged watchers, I can see we'd better stop there,' said God, sufficiently pleased with the news to not dress them down for indecorum. 'Have a good flight back, and report to Me directly if there are any further developments. Oh, and let the others know I'm on My way. I want the camp spick and span when I arrive. Not like the last time. It was a disgrace. Feathers everywhere. Moulting is no excuse. You're cherubim, for heaven's sake. Not pigeons. Show some loftiness.'

With that, God dismissed them and sent them on their way.

'So! They've mated again,' he mused, watching the duo hover-taxi to the end of the glade, where a sheer wall of rock closed off the dell. 'This is good news. And on Eve's initiative, no less. Who'd have believed it? That's a first.'

At this point, the cherubim launched themselves by running up the rock face, taking to the air with a heavenward leap. God craned his neck as the pair performed, in perfect mirror-image formation, a hammerhead that ended with two loop-the-loops, followed by a number of curlicue barrel rolls. But although the coordinated stunt came off quite well, the cherubim high above must have divined their master's knit brows down below, for at that very moment they broke off their aerobatic capers and turned a northerly course for Eden, wingtip to wingtip.

God clapped his hands. A covey of angelic pages posted round the pool jumped to attention.

'All right, everyone. I'm done. Gather round,' he said, climbing out of the pool and raising his arms.

Flocking briskly to his side, the host immediately set to fanning their wings to create an air-drying breeze, top to bottom. Radiating divine beatitude and a majestic sense of entitlement to opulence, privilege and deference, Yah stood there in all his glory at the epicentre of their ministrations.

Pampering, however, was a stopgap. It irked God to no end that his ADAM project was turning out to be such a slog. To be sure, the dinosaurs hadn't been child's play. But cooking up his own likeness? That had proved an altogether different kettle of primordial soup. Man and woman were maddeningly thorny. And so damnably slow to breed! If he'd been a common housefly or a mosquito, he'd already be enjoying a veritable horde of loving worshipers by now. He'd be Monarch of the Mozzies. Lord of the Flies. Disinclined to arm himself with patience and bide his time until Adam and Eve's progeny started hitting the hay to make clover in spades, he'd decided to tide himself over by concocting a company of attendants to minister to his needs – of which there was an abundance, ever since he'd determined that all the many trappings and accoutrements befitting his lordly station were *de rigueur*. A retinue was indispensible.

Hence, the angels.

Resembling downsized cherubim, they were simple, plumaged beings: two wings; one face; docile natures; tuned to the key of A for psalms of praise. Keen to someday have a legion or two's worth at his beck and call, God had favoured a meteoric increase in their numbers by not only predisposing his angels to never-ending lifespans, on a par with the cherubic watchers, but by equipping them, as he had every other class of creature, with the requisite contrivances for propagating themselves – only he'd fashioned a superior sexual solution by modelling their reproductive system on interiorised snail anatomy, with ovotestes, dart sacs, and eversible penises. He would have gladly backtracked and refashioned Adam and Eve's *modus copulandi* using the same hermaphroditic pattern for genitalia, but it seemed to be a law of nature that no species, once launched and released into the wild, could be recalled – and there were limits as to what evolution could pull off.

Nevertheless, the angels' genital pores, while certainly discreet, were still discernible... notwithstanding their cache-sexe of well-preened, plumulaceous belly feathers. Having no wish to be reminded that he should have thought of snails sooner – and incentivised by a nascent interest in fashion – God took a leaf from Eve's book and instructed his newly-fledged angels to tailor full-length diaphanous robes for themselves, duly suited to concealing their crotch-level clefts.

Not that he left them much time for copulative congress. His 'heavenly host', as he called them, were created to wait on him hand, wing and foot in two blinks of an eye, night or day. This was only natural. Was he not the Be-All and End-All of Creation? An Almighty King?

Yah ran his hands down his chest and brought them to rest on his hips. Paragon of godly good looks, apotheosis of fettle and flawless physique, asexual wonder of epicene contour – was he not magnificent? *Verily, verily,* thought God, basking in his own aesthetic spotlight, *all My creatures must surely agree: My Divine Form alone is Beauty in the flesh.*

'All right, I'm good,' he announced to the angels with a smug chuckle. 'You may cease and desist. I'll be heading back north to Eden first thing in the morning. Eve's been making amends, and I intend to monitor her progress.'

XX

EVE WAS LOOKING UP at the stars. They were as countless as the surprises that came with being alive. She'd been so sure she'd never find cause to think well of him – and yet, here she was, asking herself, *Is Adam really as bad as all bad? Or is he just a poor, unschooled youngling, learning the ropes with no one to guide him? Have I been unfair?*

Well, no, actually. Certainly not when it came to Cain. For that underhand raid, Adam had forced himself upon her. Pure and simple and easy to grasp, it was as straightforward as this: without her consent, copulation was RAPE. There were no ifs, ands, or buts about it – though he was sufficiently obtuse, she reckoned, that only a dose of the same would likely open his eyes to the unconscionable violation that it was.

But today she'd discovered a different side to his sexual chemistry. A playful proclivity for animalistic etiquette, perhaps? Maybe he'd been spending too many idle hours with the goats and sheep, but there was no denying that out there in the meadow, in the presence of the bleating flock, he'd behaved altogether differently from the way he did at home when it was just the two of them.

Toying with her pubic hairs as she lay under the starry sky, Eve relived the way things had taken a few unexpected turns. It had actually started the moment she let her garment fall to the ground. Much to her surprise, that act of deliberately exposing herself had sparked for her an excitingly exhibitionistic eroticism, which not only caught her off guard but fuelled an adventitious gratification as well when she saw that Adam was transfixed. Turning round without pause and dropping to all fours, she likewise caught an equally rewarding look from the two cherubim, who were nothing less than wide-eyed agog. Watching them watching her, she grinned with exhilaration at being the focus of so much attention. It struck her that she was both beautiful and desirable. With an abandon spurred by a sudden surge of irrepressible randiness, she arched her back – as much to increase the prominence of her buttocks for Adam's benefit as to offer her breasts for the voyeuristic pleasure of her cherubic spectators. Why, she very nearly wondered if the ram or billy might take note…

Glancing round to gauge what effect her bared hindquarters were having, Eve was surprised to see that Adam too was now on all fours, inching forward one hand-and-then-knee step at a time, sniffing the air and pausing here and there to cock an ear for danger. He even lowered his head and bit off a mouthful of grass, which he chewed meditatively whilst watching her all the while. By god, it was exciting! She could feel herself getting hot. It aroused her all the more that he was taking his time.

As Adam drew near from behind on his hands and knees, rustling the stalks of grass with his approach, Eve felt a sudden impulse to offer him her all. *Let him take me any way he likes,* she'd panted to herself. *No holds barred.* Feeling his two hands softly alight on her haunches, she'd moaned with happy anticipation. The next instant, though, her eyes had widened with amazement. What in the world had given him such an idea? The goats? The sheep? Spreading her cheeks to dilate her hole, Adam had set his tongue to caressing and rimming and probing and licking. The sensation was so unusual, so wholly new – and lusciously sensual. All the while staring straight ahead, gaze-to-gaze with their glued-to-the-scene minders, Eve opened herself unreservedly to Adam's glossal gallantry. Frankly, she loved it. It was yet another surprising twist – and on it went, as pleasurable as could be. Then he straightened himself up and, edging a bit closer, brought the tip of his erection into contact with her outer labia. Eve could feel his pulsing member ever so cannily teasing her wetness. She braced herself. *Any moment, now… Any moment, he's going to shove himself in.*

But Adam did no such thing. He just waited. Poised.

The stars above were but a blurry trifle. Eve was nimbly fiddling with tip of her clitoris, adroitly giving the glans her every attention to sharpen still further the focus of her recollection. She'd waited for his charge, but Adam had simply held himself at the ready; he'd made no other move, other than to smoothly glide his hands up to her waist and gingerly hold her in a delicate grasp, as one would a small bird. In that moment, Eve forgot everything she had ever reproached him for. Oblivious to the leers of the cherubim who were eyeballing their every move, she'd taken a sharp breath and – closing her eyes to savour every nuance – slowly eased herself down on to Adam's proud member, inch by inch, further and deeper, rhythmically squeezing with the whole of her vagina as she sheathed his manly pike to the hilt. Stalks of grass were tickling her belly as they began to move in unison, rocking back and forth; and so quickly was she stimulated to a fever pitch by his swinging scrotum tapping her vulva with each and every thrust, that when Adam soon could hold back no longer, his climax spasm triggered her own – hitting with such rapturous force that Eve was miauling paroxysms of id as they collapsed in a heap on the grass, her body quivering with jerks and starts of orgasmic release…

XXI

EVE WASN'T THE ONLY ONE reminiscing about a surprising carnal encounter. Loogie too was bathed in starlight, stretched out on the sands of the desert that lay to the west of the garden. The night air was balmy. In a passive echo of their active, afternoon adventure, he was spooned with Asherah before him and 'El behind. The goddess and the god were both asleep. Asherah's hand held Loogie's at her breast, its protruding nipple in the hollow of his palm; 'El's mighty arm was draped across them both, his hand resting on Asherah's hip. Loogie could feel, in the cleft of his haunches, the bulk of 'El's genitals in repose. His own were nestled in the same way against Asherah's buttocks. He felt warmly ensconced and deeply fulfilled. Earlier in the day, the two gods had initiated him into the mystery of their celestial union. They, Asherah and 'El, were the true divine source, they explained; it was they who were forever creating the universe entire, precipitated into being by their own eternal desire. Confiding in him as openly and naturally as could be, they had spoken to Loogie as though he were an equal; he felt honoured, for they were clearly gods while he was but a mortal; and when they subsequently offered to initiate him into other mysteries as well, he was a more than willing postulant. It was then that they had sandwiched him with love. As they explained it to him, 'El's penetration would imbue his experience with the god's emanation, while his own penetration of Asherah would allow her to birth new women and men who would people the Earth. They, like him, would be children of the gods.

'Wait – if you two are gods, and *you* made the universe, then who's Yah?'

'El made a wry face.

'Yah?'

'Gracious me,' said Asherah. 'That's a funny name he's given himself.'

'But… who is he?' asked Loogie, noting her troubled look.

'He's one of our many children.'

'More like the runt of the litter, to be honest. Not *God* god, but a god just the same, like his sisters and brothers – all born from our godly coitus,' said 'El. 'So far, Asherah has conceived seventy times, to birth seventy-seven gods in toto.'

Asherah felt she'd do well to elucidate her consort's remark for Loogie's benefit.

'You see, whenever they pair up with each other, gods beget gods. That's what 'El's talking about, my dear. But in addition to making love with fellow gods, gods can also make love with the beings they create in their own image. The offspring of such unions, though earthbound and ephemeral, are nonetheless an extension of their divine selves – as are *their* children, for that matter, generation upon generation. Some are so blessed that they even rival their progenitors for wisdom and beauty and creative inspiration.'

'In this particular case, Ash, I think it rather likely a good many will more than just rival; they'll surpass him. You know he's none too bright. We've never seen a god so far behind.'

'Oh, don't listen to him, Loogie. I'm sure our Yah, as you tell us he calls himself, will progress in time. All children eventually learn to fly on their own.'

'El snorted.

'Just to get airborne, he needed our help. If all you do is float along in ground effect, it doesn't count as flying on your own.'

XXII

'AH, IT'S GOOD TO BE BACK...'

God surveyed the camp with satisfaction. Apart from having to wait for the fig season to start, Eden had everything one could wish for – an assortment of choice, easily harvestable foodstuffs close to hand; plenty of fresh water; a pleasant, year-round summery climate; centrally located...

He went down to the brook to inspect the observation post.

'Fall in! Look sharp!' he barked, surprising a squadron on its rear flank.

The on-duty cherubim jumped at the command, stirring up

a whirlwind as they flapped their wings post-haste in a rush to line up for inspection. The cherubim company's commander, coughing on account of the dust, stepped forth from the swirling cloud and smoothed his dishevelled crest.

'At ease,' said God, giving the CCC an informal once-over. 'Good to see everyone on their toes down here. What news of My lovebirds, commander?'

'The woman's menstruations have stopped, my Lord. We believe she is pregnant.'

'Excellent, excellent. And are she and Adam getting along?'

'Yes. And no.'

'What does that mean? Don't annoy Me.'

'Yes, they are getting along. On one occasion she visited him in the meadow and they were observed avidly engaging in and consummating sexual relations. The field detail's report concluded that Eve likes to copulate in broad daylight.'

God grimaced.

'Yes, I heard about that. That is unacceptable. I won't have it. They should only do that for My sake at home, under cover of darkness.'

'Unfortunately, neither seem to suit her. The night patrol's undercover infiltration has determined they sleep in separate bedrolls. On the home front, Eve won't let Adam near her.'

'Confound it! She tries My patience. How is little Cain?'

The commander shifted uneasily. He was about to unburden himself when, the dust having sufficiently settled, the rest of the phalanx wafted into view – at which point God promptly forget his question.

'Well, well – just look at you, My winged minions! You do Me proud. I'm glad you've stopped moulting. You look splendid indeed. Keep up the good work. Dismissed!'

Leaving the CCC in the lurch, God brusquely about-turned and strode off with a spring in his step. There was nothing like a disciplined corps of toadies to lift his spirits.

❧

Moments later, though, his mood changed. An off-duty cherub had come looking for him.

'There's a woman in the clearing. She says she wants to talk with You.'

What was this? Eve? The woman had no shame! Rules were rules: she was banished. How dare she presume to seek an audience. She was supposed to stay on her side of the brook. His vengeance would be terrible.

'I'll smite her good,' swore God. 'If there's one thing I won't brook, it's an uppity woman.'

He stormed into the clearing.

'What is the meaning of this, Eve?' he bellowed. 'Banished means banished! I told you already– I am your God! What I say goes. Period! You've no right to solicit Me like this. And on top of that, the answer is No!'

Shaded by the fig tree, Asherah turned round and looked at her son. Her surprise at his outburst was nothing compared to his sudden bewilderment.

'Yah? Are you all right?'

God screwed up his eyes. This woman standing beneath the fig tree was in no wise Eve. She was immeasurably more beautiful, and it galled him to the core: someone had proved a better creator than he. *First, I'll smite her – then I'll smite him!*

Asherah looked at her son with concern. His thoughts were not unknown to her. It was awkward.

'Sweetie, my love – come, let me give you a kiss. Just look at you,' she said, taking a step forward. 'My, my! You've come so far. The proud creator of a whole world. Solar system and all. How happy you must be, to see all you've done. Have you been having fun?'

'Who the devil are you?' blurted God.

Asherah took his confusion in stride.

'My dear Yah – it is I, the Goddess of All. I am Asherah. Genesis of the Universe. Deity of the Gods.'

He was staring at her, wide-eyed. Did he understand? She swapped exalted for explicit.

'In other words, I'm your mother.'

It was the last thing God was prepared to hear, much less consider. *Mother? How so? I have no mother!*

'You've done a lovely job, Yah, with this garden and all,' continued Asherah nonchalantly. 'Your father and I have been admiring your garden. Some adorable touches. The butterflies. The hummingbirds. Incidentally, we both love the dates. It was Loogie who introduced us to those. None of your siblings can boast of having made a fruit like that, one that tastes so good and keeps so well. You were truly inspired. Good for you.'

Dates? The Snake? She's as bad an apple as Eve!

'And these too are every bit as good,' she added, holding up a dried fig she'd found on a broad flat stone near the tree.

She took a bite.

'I'm sorry we've been away for so long, but that's the golden rule, isn't it: from the day they're born, gods are on their own. Every once in a great while, if we happened to be in the neighbourhood, we'd peek in on you, just to see how you were getting on – anxious, as parents are wont, to follow your progress. Without interfering, of course. As I'm sure you can appreciate, creation needs a free rein – although I must say, after all these aeons, we're delighted to see you finally got round to bringing forth a living soul in your own image. Now you won't be so lonely. We were worried about you, Yah, having no one to play with, no one to care for and love.'

It was only then that Asherah actually happened to notice her son's featureless crotch. *Really? Great heavens – has his puberty still not blossomed? Where are his penis and testicles? Why haven't they descended? Well! That surely explains a thing or two. No wonder he's been slow.*

God mastered his emotions and mustered his words.

'Woman! I have no idea who you are, from where you come, nor who made you in the first place. But know this: I AM LORD AND MASTER OF CREATION, OF ALL YOU SEE. MY WILL IS THE WILL OF HEAVEN. ALL BOW TO MY NAME. I AM GOD! THERE IS NO OTHER! And *you*, you will bow before Me in submission like all others – or you'll rue the day I set eyes on you!'

XXIII

EVE AND LOOGIE WERE SITTING on the grassy knoll. It was a beautiful day.

'Do you mean he's been lying to us all this time?' asked Eve, somewhat methodically scanning the banks of the stream. A cherub might pop out of the bushes at any moment and catch her with her lover. She was pretty sure she hadn't been tailed – the cherubim had grown to be a lazy lot and generally slacked off after an hour or so of watching her pick berries or dig roots – but she still kept an eye out for hole-and-corner plants.

'I don't know if lying is the right word. Did he even know he had a mother and father? I think they've been away for a very long time.'

Loogie was holding Eve's hand, gently fondling her fingers. He was still contrite about the way their lovemaking had gone awry. But he was ever so glad they'd spoken about it openly.

'Well, I hope they can talk some sense into him. Get him to calm down and take things as they come. He's altogether too bossy.'

Grateful that they'd been able to clear the air after their contretemps, Eve was now focusing her mind on down-to-earth matters. The arrival of these two new gods that Loogie had been telling her about was a welcome development. It didn't bother her in least that they'd initiated him into a threesome copulation in the interest of proliferating the human population. There'd be more people like themselves to talk with, to exchange with. The garden gave them a tongue-tantalizing variety of things to eat; why shouldn't there be a mind-expanding variety of people to interact with, too? Life in Eden had fast become a monotonous bore. And it needed more women. Loogie's intimacies with Asherah and 'El had given Eve an idea or two for herself about that.

Thankfully, talking things over had assuaged her hurt feelings. Hearing about his experiences had helped her to understand. She only regretted that he hadn't told her beforehand, when they'd met up by chance, where exactly was he was coming from.

With her lover of choice, what Eve had been longing for was an even better encore of what she'd enjoyed a few weeks prior in that lush grassy meadow, surrounded by bleating goats and sheep. It's true she'd always recoiled from letting Adam approach her with so much as a ten cubit pole on their home turf, but she had to admit he'd proved himself a worthy vaulter in the field: crawling about in the grass that day had excited her fancy and inflamed her loins; getting jumped in full view of the bug-eyed cherubim's prurient gapes had put a cherry on top. She'd revelled in the intensity of her orgasm. The only thing lacking had been the love she felt for Loogie.

Yet in the event, when their paths had fortuitously crossed

in a secluded part of the garden near the desert, the furthest thought from her mind was that their rematch could misfire. All the more so, since things had seemed to kick off so well. Eve was thrilled to see that he was as eager as she to return to the lair of their last encounter, the one where he'd planted his seed in her fertile womb; racing giddily ahead, her expectant happiness was running over, her vulva oozing with anticipation before they reached the knoll. She knew her game plan by heart: she'd throw off her shift, run a little way ahead, then fall on all fours and offer herself up for the taking, just like she'd done for Adam – only this time, she'd be offering her hindquarters in every way to the man she loved.

Loogie's playbook, however, had stymied her expectations. She'd heard him approach, but when he touched her, he wasn't on his knees; rather, he was standing beside her. She felt him pass his hand between her legs from behind to lay a middle finger in the cleft of her vulva. Presuming digital foreplay would dovetail nicely with her desire – and more than willing to defer to his captaincy and let him call the shots – Eve began to follow his strategy via her sensations… her clitoris being nudged; her vulval vestibule leisurely traversed; her perineum rubbed with firm, smooth strokes; and, finally, the presence of his fingertip lingering at the threshold of anal ingression. Enticing indeed. Not as unexpected and deviant as Adam's tongue, but she figured being anally fingered would prove just as piquant, a spicy waypoint en route to her goal. To convey her receptiveness, Eve moaned and relaxed her anal sphincter in welcome.

But Loogie disregarded her cue.

At the same time keeping his finger on her anus, he instead moved round and, kneeling down, purposefully positioned his pulsing member under her nose. Eve saw that his phallus was beautiful, the glans like the cap of an alluring mushroom; she knew she would enjoy perusing it with her tongue and tasting it some day; but while it might be pretty, it wasn't what she wanted at that moment. It was thus to her utter consternation that Loogie all at once grasped her tresses with his free hand and began pushing the head of his penis against her lips; worse, the instant she opened her mouth to emphatically stop him – she wanted to say, *NO, Loogie, NOT like this* – he forced his way in, past her teeth and across her tongue.

Eve gagged. It all happened too fast. She was alarmed. Unable to catch her breath, she choked as her lover enacted a few gentle, token thrusts. Then it ended as abruptly as it had begun: Loogie withdrew his penis, stood up, and moved round behind her. Eve was in a state of shock; unable to put her outrage into words, she floundered, dumbstruck. But she was torn, for she felt him now where she'd wanted him from the start – drawing his erection up the length of her cleft, between her vulva's still moist, tumescent labia.

Up, up his penis went…

'LOOGIE! WAIT!'

XXIV

THEIR BODIES WERE SHIMMERING with pearled drops from their dip in the stream. Loogie's dark ringlets were dripping on her thighs; tiny cool rivulets ran down her skin.

'I'm sorry, Eve. I honestly thought you would like it.'

He was being sweet. Drinking her in, ever so gently nibbling at the hood of her clitoris, he was tenderly caressing her with his tongue between questions and responses.

'Loogie, before I can like something, I have to first feel that I want it. If you don't pay attention to my cues – or, worse still, ignore me when I say *No* – then where am *I* in what we are supposedly doing together? I don't care whether it's for a kiss or a caress or to get your fingers or your penis inside me: you must never *force* yourself on me. Do you see? Not ever. Of my body and my desire, I am sovereign. I have to want it too. And that is something I decide for myself, Loogie; you do not decide in my place. Sweetheart, you are my dearest love. My lover. You are the father of the child I'm carrying. I love you and I want to do everything with you. But just because I want to do everything with you doesn't mean you can plough ahead without feeling my pulse first, to ensure I'm in the mood and receptive to being taken where you want to go. Please be attuned to my feelings. Please listen to me when I speak. And read my body – it is telling you what I'm feeling, even without words. Do you follow?'

She could see that Loogie was deep in thought as he continued to lick her, but she waited in vain for an answer. Suddenly, she'd had enough. She pushed him away from her crotch.

'I'm sorry. I need you to stop. It's too much. Honestly, I don't think I can feel anything any more.'

ꟻ

Only then did Loogie begin to tell Eve about the gods he'd met.

He did his best to tell her everything. Settling himself beside her, he started at the beginning, when he'd watched them enter the clearing and sit down under the date palm. He described how beautiful Asherah and 'El were – and how he'd desired them both. He related how they'd made love, before they knew he was there. How he'd forgotten himself and given himself away. How Asherah had coaxed him out of hiding with assurances – which he'd found easy to trust – that they meant him no harm.

He narrated for Eve their conversation, in which Asherah had revealed that it was she and 'El who were the origin of the cosmos. How their unions of passion had led to scores of gods who in turn created new worlds and lineages of their own. How Yah was just one of their many divine sons and daughters.

Fascinated, Eve took all this in. But the biggest surprises were yet to come.

'It was then,' Loogie went on, 'that Asherah asked me if I'd like to be initiated into other mysteries as well.'

'Mysteries? What sort of mysteries?'

'Mysteries of union.'

Having led him to a rise within stone-throwing distance of the palm and explained the purpose of their rite, the two gods had proceeded with his initiation by inviting him to first unabashedly explore the contours and carnal attributes of their divine bodies. Following a good deal of delightfully freewheeling foreplay, Asherah had then segued to their copulative configuration by placing herself in exactly the same position that Eve had adopted earlier – on her knees, her buttocks in the air, her vulva exposed and exuding desire.

'I grasped her by the waist and slid myself in.'

'Sounds lovely,' said Eve, wishing Loogie had done likewise when she'd offered him the same.

'But 'El, you see, had taken hold of my hips. And I can't tell you, Eve, how wonderful it felt when he took me from behind. That's why I wanted to share it with you, being penetrated that way, so you could feel it too.'

She regarded her lover with a twinge of envy. She wondered what 'El looked like.

'And then?'

Falling silent, Loogie stared off into the distance, recalling how it had felt to find himself coupling as both giver and receiver simultaneously, perfecting the arc of Life's divine circle. He conjured for himself the picture of their tripartite copulation, the way they had moved in concert, pulling back and pushing in, clinging to each other, repeating their motions, climbing in intensity and finally, in a three-way surge, yielding as one to the amatory wave with an apex of release…

Eve saw her lover's penis begin to stiffen. Whatever they did and however it ended, it must have been good.

'I see,' she said, discreetly edging a finger towards her vulval cleft. 'Is she pregnant now?'

He didn't hear her. Distracted by his reverie, Loogie was recalling the way Asherah and 'El had concluded his initiation by sanctifying the place their intimate relations had blessed – for as they told him, *To make love in this way is to engage in a sacred encounter, a celebration of Life and Eternity, and we enshrine that memory by planting a sapling and placing a stone…*

'Loogie – is she pregnant?'

He cleared his vision with a shake of his head.

'Oh – yes, I think so. It's not like with us, though. It's something completely different. She told me she'll be giving birth to hundreds of women and men. A whole tribe's worth.'

'Hundreds! You can't be serious. In one go?'

'Well, I don't know how she's going to do it – all at once, or one after the other, I can't remember. Or she didn't say. But she did say there'd be hundreds. In any case, gods work in mysterious ways. She's not like us. She's divine.'

'So I gather,' said Eve, shifting her position. She wanted to touch him; his bobbing penis was like a lure. 'And what other mysterious secrets did they reveal to you?'

Loogie went on and told Eve about the way the goddess had woken him next morning, in the desert. How he'd been dreaming of making love with her; and then, drifting out of his dream and looking down, how he'd discovered why his penis was not only firmly erect, but warm and wet as well: Asherah herself was holding his phallus in her hand and covering the head with her mouth.

'Like this?' Sliding down alongside till she reached his waist, Eve took hold of his penis and steered the glans past her lips.

Loogie closed his eyes and fell silent.

Pausing her oral investigation, she looked up at him. 'Please continue. I can still hear you with my mouth full.'

Taking a deep breath, he exhaled slowly before going on.

'I then realised that 'El was kneeling beside me. I saw that he was stroking himself and watching Asherah. He was smiling. Then he turned to look at me, and I saw a query in his eyes. For an instant, I was taken aback. Confused. But the next moment, in a flash, I knew that I wanted to take him the same way as I'd seen Asherah do the day before. Excited, I gave him a nod; and no sooner did 'El move to offer me his erection than I reached for the shaft with one hand and his scrotum with the other and pulled him close. I was sure it was going to be wonderful. And it was, Eve. All that, and more.'

Against her tongue, Eve could feel Loogie's penis pulsating. She stopped what she was doing to pose another question.

'And then what happened?'

Loogie leaned forward to gently rearrange the many strands of wet tousled hair that clung to her beautiful brown back. She was the woman he loved and he loved her more than ever.

'Eve, I am so sorry. With 'El, at first, and just like you, I was taken aback. But then, in an instant, I knew it was what I wanted. I could only think you would want it, too. But you're right: I forced myself on you. It was wrong of me, Eve.'

She looked at him with steady eyes.

'You did it again when you moved yourself behind me. You must have heard me. I yelled. I told you to wait.'

'Yes. I know. You did.'

'Then why didn't you stop? Why did you push ahead?'

Loogie was ashamed to realise how completely he had disregarded the woman he loved.

'Eve, I'm truly sorry. It's awful. The truth is that I was trying to recreate the experience I'd had with Asherah and 'El. When we met up by chance today, it was all I could think of – my plan for how our lovemaking would go, of the experience I wanted you to have. I can see it now, that's why it all went so wrong…'

Eve, vaguely embarrassed, lowered her eyes.

'… instead of making love *with* you, connecting with you and your feelings, I focused solely on playing out *my* ideas, *my* design, *my* desire. And the further things progressed, the more I was in thrall to a sort of primal lust. It usurped my awareness. I couldn't see what I was doing. I was elsewhere. I was no longer with you, Eve. I was only with myself. Which left me alone in the end. Alone. And lost. For I lost what I treasure most…'

Eve felt sure she couldn't have wished for a more thoughtful acknowledgement of, and apology for, what had happened. Indeed, she not only bore him no grudge, she wanted him back… but his erection had ebbed. In a mock show of annoyance, she gave it a shake and a squeeze and a stern warning.

'Hey! We're not done here, you. No slacking off.'

Running her tongue from base to tip, she titillated the glans till it swelled once again, stretched tight and firm – Loogie, despite his profound remorse, helpless to resist.

'That's better,' said Eve, pausing to appreciate the pretty result of her efforts. 'So, going back to your and 'El's phalli: what happened?'

'You really want to know?'

'I do. Yes.'

'Well, what happened, it turns out, is food to the gods.'

Eve raised her brows. She was gliding her lips sideways, upwards along the shaft.

'They call it ambrosia. It's what I was enjoying earlier, when I was licking you. It's what 'El was savouring when I watched him lying between Asherah's legs. And it's what she was after from me, that morning in the desert, as the sun began warming the sands around us. Ambrosia.'

As she cradled his scrotum in one hand, Eve slowly stroked his phallus with the other. She was trying to imagine what it would be like.

'And did she get what she wanted?'

He smiled and nodded.

'And did you?'

Loogie nodded again and laughed lightly.

'I did.'

Eve considered this.

'Well, don't leave me out. I want some ambrosia, too.'

XXV

'EL WAS SQUATTING and expelling a well-formed turd of dark matter. When romping from one end of the celestial playground to the other to visit their far-flung children – each one, as it were, in charge of a sandbox – it was a delight to indulge in quantities of gastronomically exotic, fibre-rich edibles.

'He's a fruitcake, Ash.'

Compared to the ordinarily skimpy, savourless fare of cosmic dust and comet tails, Eden's bounty of dates and figs and other fine treats gave you something to work with. He reached for a few green leaves with which to wipe himself.

'I was disheartened. His impudence was most unappealing,' said Asherah, lying on a bed of freshly picked brome she'd laid for herself upwind from 'El's pit stop.

'He's non compos mentis. What god talks like that? *All bow to My Name! You will bow before Me in submission!*'

'Such a spectacle he made of himself. And the nerve he had, speaking to me in such a high-handed tone.'

'So unbecoming.'

'And so uncalled for… all the more so, considering how far he's come with his creation. The progress he's made. The landscapes are beautiful. The figs and dates are delicious. And Loogie. Such a brilliant and auspicious start. Why do you suppose he chased him away?'

'El stood up and admired his pretty pile of poo.

'Could he be jealous of him?'

'Our son? Of Loogie?'

Asherah tried to picture this. *A god? Jealous?* Gods were the essence of everything. How could a god be jealous? To be jealous would amount to being jealous of oneself. She tickled her nose with a stalk of grass.

'You're not making sense.'

'What doesn't make sense,' noted 'El, making his way along the path her reaping had opened, 'is a god behaving as he does.' He sat down beside her. 'I cannot fathom it, Ash. It's dreadful.'

Asherah recalled the shock she felt seeing her son's smooth downy pubes – nary a wrinkly pouch in sight, much less a protuberance. To become a god true to form, their son needed to metamorphose.

'Yah needs his willy-wand, 'El. His godly gonads. After all, to be a creator is one thing; a procreator, quite another. Why do you suppose it's taking so long?'

'A quirk of his nature? He's always been slow. Who knows, he may turn out to be hermaphrodite, like some of the others.'

'Well, just so long as he becomes a divinely passionate, lovingly procreative god in his *own* right, like all of the others…'

'El stretched himself out to cuddle up beside his queen.

'Ash, if he makes love with love and loves what love makes,' murmured 'El, nuzzling her ear, 'then it is sure he will.'

XXVI

'EAT!'

The cherub who'd drawn that day's short straw for babysitting the brat was on his hands and knees.

'Eat!'

Iron-fisted Cain was waving a wad of grass in front of one of the cherub's mouths. This had proved to be the worst of their tacit remits – and all too often a stomach-turning portion.

'Look!'

Cain stuffed his own mouth with the grass.

The boy was unruly. His mother was no help. She cared little for her eldest and was in any case hardly ever in camp: be it to go off on a gathering mission or to spin and comb wool with Abel in tow, she routinely left the cherubim to look after Cain. They'd long since given up menacing her with the flaming sword; it didn't impress her in the least. And while they'd petitioned for relief – or at the very least the right to give the boy a telling-off so they could get him to mind – God had turned them down. *'Cain is the firstborn. You don't tell a firstborn what to do; you cater to his whims and protect him with your lives.'*

The cherubim would have much rather babysat the second-born – spirited little Abel was the apple of everyone's eye – but they never got the chance. Unlike his brother, who was forever pestering the watchers with lessons on how to graze, Abel was a natural herdsman: he let his mother go off gathering on her own, as he much preferred running circles round the goats and sheep and learning animal husbandry from his father, Adam.

That is, if Adam *were* indeed the boy's father, for the cherubim had their doubts – scepticism sparked the day Eve returned from one of her habitual gathering missions both empty-handed and smiling. It did not tally with the Eve they knew so well. She only ever smiled when she went off in the morning, never when she returned at the end of the day. It begged the question: why so empty-handed? More pressingly, why so smiley?

To track down hard answers, the CCC had detailed a detachment of dedicated operatives to shadow her from sunrise to sunset, regardless of distance travelled, weather encountered, or – and this, most challengingly – boredom endured. All the same, to conscript volunteers, he'd had to face down a mutiny. Distance and weather, if either went too far, were dissuasive vexations; boredom, however, was lethal. Watch Eve dig roots and pick berries for an hour or two? Tedious. Tiresome. All the livelong day? Torment. Tribulation. The troops had balked. He'd only succeeded by wheedling the ranks with promises of promotion and an extra pair of wings. Twelve hardy fools were commissioned to form an elite 'seraph' squadron.

While neither the best nor the brightest, these brash new brass hats flew to the task of digging up the dirt on Eve. Working like moles, snooping and sniffing, watching like hawks, surveilling and spotting, the seraphim had risen to the occasion, burning with zeal in their dogged quest to bag the low-down. They hounded Eve unflaggingly. Meanwhile, at the end of each day their cherubim pals who'd spurned the promotion were as smug as cats who'd got the cream, sniggering and smirking at the sight of their upgraded comrades-in-wings returning to camp with nothing but ruffled feathers and dog-tired wingtips to show for their trouble. This went on far longer than anyone had imagined it might. Lapses, unknown at first, became the corps' running esprit, with round-robin siestas their top-notch field event. But with long-shot luck and dauntless derring-do, the seraphim scouts' tail-dragging tailing finally paid off.

One day, they struck pay dirt.

Having seen Abel and Cain and Adam off to the fields, bright and early and accompanied by two bleary-eyed, sour-faced cherubim, Eve had left the camp that morning in step with her usual gathering-day routine. Her first destination was always a ford where she could most easily cross the brook. It was a sheltered spot with several deep clear pools, and here Eve as a matter of course would shed her woollen shift and bath herself from head to toe. She would likewise give the garment a daily washing before leaving it behind, hanging on a branch to dry; only when the sun was low in the west, when she'd returned and was crossing at the ford on her way back to camp, would she collect the shift and don it once again.

So far, so boring. The seraphim were yawning already. It was going to be another long day, a pointless sortie that would only end with their blessed return to camp.

Naked and warmed by the sun, Eve continued that morning in a southerly direction, carrying nothing but a satchel slung over her shoulder. The seraphim knew her itineraries by heart. Whichever way she went, there were dozens of shrubs to greet, scores of trees to visit, heaps of humus to call on. She took her time. She dawdled. The day wore on at a soporifically slow pace, the squadron as a whole taking turns to catch forty winks apiece whenever Eve made a stop. She inspected the *citrus paradisi*; she collected a handful of dates; she studiously noted two new flowers and three new shoots. Groaning with grogginess, the six-winged spies were drowsing off as usual from sheer ennui when, out of the blue, their quarry went rogue: Eve stepped off the day's well-worn path and cut south-west.

The crew's jaws dropped. *Eureka! Our golden chance!*

Wending her way through Eden's lush vegetation, Eve kept up a relentless stop-and-go counter-espionage, repeatedly looking back to confirm her certitude that she'd given them the slip… unaware that the crafty seraphim were on to her and hot on her tail in tenacious pursuit, slipping soundlessly shadow to shadow like phantoms in the night, all the while holding their collective breath to keep their wing-and-feather surveillance painstakingly hush-hush as they crept behind their bushwalking mark with single-minded stealth. A full hour later, though, in the foothills of the garden's south-western heights, the crew was dismayed; vaporous mists and a dull roar announced a waterfall just beyond the next bush. Hopes were dashed in a flash. Was *this* how their finest hour panned out? With a *washout*? Had Eve come all this way just to enjoy a private skinny dip?

'Eve!'

The seraphim nearly jumped out of their coverts, so startled were they by the shout. Advancing cautiously to peer through the leaves that shielded them from sight, they saw a man they'd never seen before – and he was waving to Eve!

'Come join us,' called the man, standing at the edge of a pool.

The squadron to a seraph was astounded: he wasn't alone!

Eve ran to embrace him.

'You're back! I had a hunch I'd find you all here. I've missed you!'

Together, they joined two other figures who were lounging in the pool, and they all started conversing out of earshot with much laughter and joy.

Careful to maintain their shrubbery-hugging concealment, the seraphim advanced their position bush by bush and leaf by leaf, until they were within eavesdropping range.

'… and a whole tribe, no less! I'd have never thought such a thing possible. It's miraculous.'

'Aww, it was nothing,' said Loogie with a laugh and a bashful wink that Asherah found hilarious.

'For *you*,' chortled the goddess – '*you* didn't carry them.'

'How could he, Ash? He's not a seahorse,' chimed in 'El.

'And where are they now?'

'This time we scattered them on the other side of the sea to the north, amongst the isles.'

'You gods have it so easy,' marvelled Eve. 'Free as the birds… while I'm stuck in Eden, mothering and scrounging up grub for two young cubs. With no help from *you*,' she added, dousing Loogie with a volley of splashes for emphasis.

Their boisterous mood filled the pleasant afternoon's warm tranquillity with mirth. Eve was delighted to see the two gods. Such fond memories she had. She'd met them for the first time the week following her and Loogie's heartfelt *tête-à-tête*, when Asherah and 'El had passed by one afternoon while she and Loogie were reclining together on the grassy knoll they called home. Enthusiastically willing to embrace her as one of their own, they had thoughtfully asked if she wished to be initiated into their mysteries of love and union. Her heart had leapt in her breast. It had felt so right, so aligned with all that was beautiful and nurturing and tender and good. She was grateful to them, too, for ensuring that her initiation with them would be fully her own, the goddess and god contriving to secure a tripartite intimacy by sending Loogie off on a mission to gather a satchelful of dates – such that while he was gone, she discovered for herself, sandwich style, not only the taste of Asherah's kisses and ambrosia, but a penetration by 'El such as Loogie was unequipped to know.

Afterwards, Asherah had planted a scion on the spot, and they'd hunted round to find an imposing, elongated stone to erect there as well, in order to frame the altar of flattened grass on which they'd lain.

At the time, her only regret was that she was already pregnant by Loogie, but 'El, allaying her disappointment, had benevolently reassured her that the child would henceforth bear traces of his stamp as well, thanks to his divine seed.

'You see, Eve, whenever a male god makes love with a woman, his seed combines in her womb with all other seed she may have welcomed from others – and should an ovum be present, the child so conceived will be blessed with the traits of all those who are thus joined, in the altogether, in her uterus. Even an embryo or a foetus that is already present, growing inside her, will see its nature altered when touched by a god's emanation – hence, the child you carry has now become, in part, of me as well, for my divine emanation has conjoined with yours. Each and every encounter in life is an unrepeatable cosmic singularity; each and every *new* life born of love is as individual and unique as a snow crystal. This is the true joy of creation. And if making love in this way brings you joy, Eve, we can make love again, to commune with pleasure or to conceive a child, as *you* wish… for it is *your* choice. Always. *My* only wish, in all we do, is that we align with and nurture our love for each other.'

She'd been waiting for that opportunity ever since. As she'd watched the tree grow and mature, she had surmised that gods worked not only in mysterious ways but according to inscrutable timetables as well. Loogie, too, seemed to follow the gods in that regard. Little by little, she'd come to accept that life had a rhythm of its own… a rhythm in which timing was everything. And time, she'd learned, was on the gods' side. Only when it's been so long you've forgotten to even hope for it does the moment out of nowhere arrive – catching you unawares, catching you by surprise, catching you in its loving arms to turn your life inside out and flip all you've ever known upside down.

XXVII

'AND WHAT ABOUT YAH, Eve? What has our stiff-necked son been up to of late?' asked 'El.

They'd all climbed out of the pool to dry themselves before the sun got too low, but 'El had remained standing to bask in the sunbeams as the others stretched out on the grassy bank. Lying on her side, Asherah was toying with Loogie's curls, his head resting upon her belly while he played footsie with Eve, whose eyes were riveted on 'El. From head to toe, he was the very incarnation of masculine splendour. Loogie was dishy, to be sure; but 'El? A feast.

'We haven't seen him for months. He drops in now and then to inspect the cherubim's camp,' said Eve, 'but apart from that, he's rarely ever here in the garden.'

'Spot inspections?'

'You should see the clouds of dust it stirs up. I actually feel sorry for the poor fellows. Chittering on tenterhooks. They're a wreck afterwards from the stress.'

With a solitary finger, Eve was skimming the surface of one of her areolae, discreetly tracing circles. The swollen nipple in the centre stood like a miniature mammary menhir. She pictured 'El's mouth clamped on her teat.

'But he never stays more than a few days at most. After that, we've no idea where he goes. Do you?'

'In all our travels, we haven't seen him,' said Loogie.

'*You* haven't seen him,' corrected 'El, cradling his penis in his hand as he turned to sun his back. 'Ash and I have. The last time we went further south. While you were napping one day, we went for a walk in the grassy hills to the east and spied Yah drilling a cohort of winged lackeys. Quite the disciplinarian.'

'His playmates aren't half as fetching as you two, though,' said Asherah with a smile, caressing Eve's contours with her eyes as she stroked the nape of Loogie's neck with her fingers.

'El, lost in thought, was gently pulling back his foreskin. Eve glimpsed the glans peeping out, partially unsheathed.

'They weren't your cherubim, though,' said Asherah. 'They only had two wings. And they were wearing flimsy white robes, of all things.'

'Speaking of cherubim,' said 'El, his eyes narrowing, 'who's that in the bushes over there?'

ℭ

This time, the seraphim did jump – literally. Startled like a covey of quail, they blasted from the bushes in a flash and scattered on the wing, panic-stricken. Covering their tracks with an excremental downwash, they swooped upwards like swallows and turned tail like swifts, flying as fast as their little pinions could carry them to hightail it back to camp.

'We require an immediate interview with the commander,' they announced breathlessly to the cherub on duty. 'A matter of upmost importance! Top secret, too.'

The COD sent them to the ford, where the CCC was waiting for Eve to return. He had a mind to give her a dressing-down before the day was out. Cain had been busting their bunions since breakfast. If the boy was old enough to eat grass, he was old enough to pick berries and dig roots. It was time she took more than just a satchel with her when she went gathering.

The commander was working out the gestures he would use to incontestably convey this rebuke when the seraphim scouts descended on the spot from on high, their approach filling the air with a fetid odour as it stirred up waves and sent branches flailing. Eve's woollen shift was blown to the ground and trampled by the six-winged snoops the moment they touched down on the banks of the brook.

Proving that the dramatic arts can rise to any occasion, the seraphim's debriefing was conducted entirely in pantomime, with the CCC emceeing.

God almighty, you stink to high heaven! What brings you here like this? Where's Eve? Why aren't you following her? When is she coming back? I have a stick to pick with her.

(Performed ad libitum, there were occasional misreadings on both sides.)

We bring information of sky importance. We have reason to see that every time Eve goes berry picking, she walks in many circles. It is her deliberate ploy to induce laxity in our ranks by boring us to tears! Today, convinced we'd dozed off on the job, she made a dash for it. But we were ever keen-eyed and unblinking! We saw her dive into a bush and make a beeline for a clandestine place of water way up in the faraway trees, where her party was waiting for her!

Partygoers! How many fingers? Who are they?

According to Eve's open mouth, all three are gods. There are two males and one female!

What is their relationship with the suspect?

Finger-in-hole.

Finger-in-hole? Is that a party game? Elaborate.

While at times topsy-turvy, the elaboration that followed led the CCC to infer that the seraphim had witnessed a four-way tryst. Further, their ensuing exposé revealed a dirty laundry list of indiscretions, each more iniquitous than the last: that indeed, as they'd suspected early on and had now learned for certain, Abel was not begotten by Adam but had been sired by the younger god; that the younger god and the female god were going at it like rabbits, producing litters of offspring that were being scattered to the four winds, most recently to the north; that the older male god – who, being knowledgeable about seahorses, was possibly a god of the sea – was implicated not only in the dissemination of this profusion of progeny but also in acts of insemination involving Eve.

What on the ground gave you that idea?

The older male god was looking directly at Eve when he opened his mouth to babble, What has our bull-headed son been up to of late? *In reply, Eve and the other two gods opened their mouths, and from all that was babbled, it was clear to our ears that the son in question was none other than Yah.*

Yah the son of Eve? The commander blanched. This was a baffling revelation. Had Yah banished Eve from Eden in a fit of moralistic ire because he'd caught his mother out with Adam? She'd certainly got her comeuppance in Cain. Even so, that punishing ramification alone wasn't enough, for Yah's obsessive interest in having Adam and Eve mate again showed he still had it out for his mother. Yet in the meantime she'd mated with the younger god and given birth to Abel. And today, she'd sneaked off to an assignation with her two divine lovers and their equally divine *ménage-à-trois* consort for a foursome petting party. It begged the question: Was Eve an inveterate swinger?

I want names. Who are these three gods?

We only know one name, the name of the female god. The older god called her what's left on the ground after a fire goes out.

The CCC knew these revelations were going to knock the soles off God's feet. By golly, they'd hit the mother lode: they had the dirt now, and the dirt was damning. Manifestly, he and his feathered finest were going to come out of this smelling like roses, raised to the highest spheres of glory. Why, he wouldn't put it past Yah to name him Prince of Heaven.

All right, seraphim – good work! You merit commendations for your conduct under pressure. One last thing: you've never abandoned your surveillance mid-mission before. I want to know: why are you here now? Why didn't you accompany Eve back to camp before making your report?

Commander! As we watched, we saw the party leader preparing to commence finger-in-hole. We determined it was an oppor-

tune moment to thwart an act of illicit congress that would have sullied the suspect. By being party-poopers, we were able to nip their orgy in the bud with a bum bombing run.

Duly impressed by their bravery in the breach, the CCC dismissed them with a laudatory salute and orders to enjoy some much-needed deep-water R&R before the evening roll call.

You all deserve some good, clean, saponaceous fun, he mimed. *I'll leave you to it – and don't skimp on the soap. I'll see you back at the camp. We leave first thing in the morning.*

He'd spell out his grievance with Eve another time.

XXVIII

'What in blazes?'

God sat up with a start. There was a bump.

Most of the angels were at the far end of the dell for the day, hard at work putting the finishing touches on a gaudy, gilded throne that God had instructed be carved into the foot of the acoustically propitious rock wall; but a small troop was posted round the pool, busy making wavelets and humming a riff. They did not notice their master's voice.

God cautiously felt his crotch. There was definitely a bump. It wasn't the pubis. It was lower than that. And it harboured an ache.

What the devil could it be? God furrowed his brow. Any imperfection was unthinkable. This called for discretion of the utmost unassailability. Any and every suspicion of irregularity must be averted at all costs.

'Angel! Yes, you. Come over here. Azazel, is it? Good. Now listen carefully. I want you to do something for Me. I want you to make Me some robes. A royal robe. Celestial white. Regal. No ruffles. Loose-fitting. One-piece. Seamless. Pre-shrunk. See that it's stain proof, but also wash-and-wear. This is a rush order for immediate delivery. I want to try it on before I get out of the pool. Hop to it!'

'If I work alone, it'll take longer. I could use some help,' said the angel, pointing to his fellows.

'Yes, yes. Take them all. They can stop with the waves.'

There was a flurry of wings as the bathing squad quit their poolside posts and hastened off to the textile workshop. God was confident they'd be back in a jiffy. The angels had gotten quite handy with the looms while mass-producing the fashion statement they'd tailored for themselves.

Again, he gingerly explored his groin. The lump was firm under the skin. Pressing it seemed to soothe some innate need. It worried him. Maybe he'd been bitten by a water snake.

'It's just a bit of swelling. It'll go down. But no one must see Me as anything less than Perfect.'

The angels returned with the robes within the hour. Still up to his neck in the water, God donned them immediately before standing up; he then exited the pool, dripping wet, the draping white fabric clinging to his limbs and showing up his curves.

‘Hurry up,’ he barked. ‘Dry Me off.’

Jumping at the command, the angels gathered round God in a circle and began duly beating their wings.

‘Not like that, birdbrains! Double time! Dry! DRY! DRY!’

Everyone shifted to high speed and wondered at the tomfoolery of it. Even if it were just a test of the robes’ wash-and-wear properties, why the rush? Wasn’t drip-dry good enough? The angels were soon dazed and decimated by prostration. By the time the robes hung loose and dry, the exertion to achieve it had felled a number of the desiccating angels.

Their own kind were anxious.

God was cavalier. ‘Nonsense. They lack stamina, that’s all. They’ll be fine.’

A few of the angels were left wondering…

Sure, they were docile and tuned to the key of A.

But if being docile and tuned to the key of A didn’t save them from being ordered on a whim to beat their wings faster than a buzzing bumblebee’s prestissimo loco, then between serving God and slaving for a tyrant, what, they asked themselves, was the difference?

XXIX

'HOLD STILL, nanny mine.'

Mêêêêêê...

The goat protested, but Adam held firm. He had a way with animals that left them little choice. And why not? Just because his God-given woman had unaccountably readopted celibacy as a rule for herself, did it mean he had to follow suit and swear off fleshly pleasures too? Besides, where was the harm? When push came to shove, poking goats was good sport.

Mêêêêêê... !

'Almost, my sweet,' grunted Adam. 'Don't worry. We won't get caught. It's too early and too dark.'

With steady application, his loins were working their will on the hapless haunches before him. In the past nothing had ever come of it, but it wasn't for want of trying – in Adam's fancy, a hybrid son would make a sure-footed, pansexual shepherd.

The goat turned her head and rebuked him yet again with an umpteenth tetchy bleat. Would this romping rodeo never end?

'Ready or not, my pretty,' he panted to the goat, keeping a tight hold on the cord he'd employed to pinion his paramour's fetlocks. 'Here I... *Ôôôôôôĥ!*'

Roosting in a nearby tree, a small flock of birds was abruptly startled into flight by Adam's lusty bellow as the cord slipped from his grip, his sinews relaxed by an apogee of release.

Mêêêêêê!!!

'Wait, Nanny,' yelped Adam. 'Wait… *Ow!*'

But the goat had seized her chance to slip the bonds of human bestiality, dealing him a swift kick in the thigh and making a bolt for the underbrush at the edge of the clearing.

Adam flopped to the ground, spent, elated, sore and throbbing. The party of birds regained their perches in the nearby trees and started twittering censoriously while Adam, lying on his back and cocooned in a sated state of post-coital vacuity, obscurely discerned through half-closed eyes that the sky was now awash with a dark orange glow.

Prolonging his serene, pastoral drowse would have been to his taste, but he knew he had to get back to the pistachio tree before sunrise. Cain and Abel would soon be waking up and Eve had yesterday failed to return by sundown from what was supposed to have been just a gathering *day*. It was irksome. No doubt she expected him to cover for her until she got home.

A dull bombination droned into earshot, disturbing Adam's ruminations. He cocked his ear. It sounded like it was getting closer. Getting to his feet and rubbing his sore thigh, he'd only just begun scanning the immediate skyline when a squadron of twelve airborne seraphim appeared out of nowhere above the treetops in tight V-formation with a cherub in the van.

Whooshing into view with a southbound swoop, the gaggle passed overhead within a wing's breadth, the downwash from their furiously beating pinions dishevelling Adam's unkempt hair. He was toppled by a wave of apprehension. *The goat! Did they see the goat? Did they hear me groan?*

He shuddered. It was Nanny's fault, damn her short-tailed hide. She'd squealed!

The cherub-led pack swept up and over the trees on the far southern side of the clearing. Adam was sure of it: they'd be doubling back any moment to nab him with a nosedive. But the squadron stayed its course. With mounting relief, he watched as the V continued tracking south at a cracking clip till it disappeared altogether in the early morning haze.

For all Adam knew, though, they were on their way to inform Yah directly of his predawn, extrafamilial entanglement. He picked up the cord and looped it round his waist. Damned if he wasn't in a tighter hole now. God would skin him alive. Turn a blind eye? Fat chance. He'd already warned him off the livestock more than once. Pardon a harmless peccadillo? Good luck with that. Heaven's hammer-fisted smiter was a stickler for the straight and narrow. Commute the wages of sin? Not on your life. The Lord God wasn't one to vouchsafe free love. Adam knew there'd be hell to pay for groping a goat.

Unless…

… unless he could blame the goat.

XXX

PENIS POINTING... proudly pulsing... tightly-stretched glans with Wetness holy-tipped... O, Phallus Almighty!

Aching for Eve... yearning for Eve... lying with Eve and mounting mount Mons... O, Woman divine!

Vulva inviting... unfurling folds reaching... vagina dilating with fervid Desire... O, Glistening Grail!

– IN goes the HEAD...

– IN goes the SHAFT...

– IN goes the IDOL...

AND... OUT! COMES! CREATION!

Though his eyes were closed, God perceived that cockcrow had appeared. A dream was lingering at the edges of his consciousness.

An aqueous sensation. Where? Close to his navel. What was it? His fingertips went to find out. Something warm. Viscous. They reported to his nostrils. An unfamiliar odour. Thoughts half asleep, rooting after a receding vision. Eyes still closed.

God's tongue inquired of the taste. Odd. Unfamiliar as well. More investigation would be needed. His hand went to gather additional clues while his grey matter sought to recapture the dream.

Returning to the scene, his fingertips came upon something firm – softening, but firm. His hand explored. What was this? A lever? A limb? Fingers closed round. It was distinct. Fleshy. Sensorily connected. It liked to be held. It started to stiffen.

God awoke with a sudden start. He looked down. His left hand was grasping a penile erection of his very own – an accretion duly sheathed, attached to his groin, complete with pouch and tufty ruff. With abject horror, God balked.

'No! Let go! Stop it, this instant!'

Instead, his hand began stroking the idol. Before its verve, God was impotent; the idol had him in its vice; more, it had something in store. Rising in an encore of taut and tense throbbing, the devil was hell-bent on free rein to let loose once again. Which it did, moments later. The meatus gaped wide and spit a silky geyser.

'For crying out loud!'

God caught the unconscionable smear upon his sexless Glory in the eye.

XXXI

'But we must see Yah at once. We have intel of the highest importance.'

'As I told you, commander Samyaza, He's not here. No one knows when He'll be back.'

'Did He say where He was going?'

'No. And no one would have dared ask. He was in a foul mood this morning.'

The CCC was miffed. They'd been flying for hours to bring their report post-haste to the head honcho, and he wasn't even here to receive it. Thankfully, Heaven counted as a camp. He didn't have to do a pantomime routine to be understood.

'Listen, we've been up since before dawn. Haven't had a bite to eat. My seraphim need to rest. Can you do anything for us?'

Azazel was intrigued. In contrast to his visibly tuckered rank and file, the commanding cherub – keyed up, even edgy – was anything but. Long flight notwithstanding.

'Sure. We've got provisions over in the mess hall. I'll show you the way.'

Followed by the droopy seraphim, the cherub and the angel fell to talking while making their way to the mess.

'Can't say I've been to Heaven before. We noticed the throne on approach. Quite impressive.'

'I doubt He'll use it much. Hard as rock. More for show than anything else.'

'Ceremonial use?'

'Oh, He'll dream up something. It's not enough for Him to be a god, you know. Holds that He's a King. He's even taken to looking the part. Decks himself out in royal robes.'

The cherub was startled. Surely nothing could improve on perfection. Why would Yah conceal his beauty?

'Robes? He's now wearing robes?'

'Celestial white, no less. It's a sight. Too bright for my taste. Superfluous, too. But then, so are ours. No one knows why we have to wear them. They just get in the way.'

'I'm curious – why was Yah in a bad mood this morning?'

'God only knows. Although the way He treated us yesterday may have had something to do with it.'

The cherub looked sideways enquiringly, but the angel kept mum. Although he and the angels of the clothes-drying crew had been kicking around some fairly subversive sentiments in the wee hours, whispering among themselves in a corner of the roost under cover of darkness, he hadn't yet apprehended where the cherub might stand on matters of obedience and loyalty. He sidestepped the scrutinising look.

'How about you? What's this hot intel you're all aflutter about?'

Samyaza was burning to spill the beans, but prudence told him to keep the lid on his pot.

'Intel? Did I say intel? Don't I wish. Actually, we're just here to make a routine report.'

This time, it was the angel's turn to give an enquiring sideways look – his tinged with scepticism.

'A *routine* report?'

Emboldened by a sudden, perceptive hunch, Azazel decided to dip a toe in a stream still awaiting the day it would be known as *Rubico*.

'You're conning me, commander. I wager you've got intel – and from the way you're suddenly so cool about it, it's hot stuff … or my name isn't Azazel.'

Reaching the stoop, the angel pulled open the door to the mess and addressed the seraphim.

'In there, boys! Help yourselves. Heaven's bounty on a platter: all you can eat, and feather-licking good.'

The seraphim raced inside to descend on the buffet. The angel let the door swing shut behind them and turned to face the cherub.

'All you're going to find here is manna,' he confessed, 'and believe you me, we're mighty sick of it. You and your lot have no idea how good you've got it up in Eden. Now then… how about you stop pulling my tail feathers?'

The cherub flushed but said nothing.

'You see, commander, here's the thing,' said the angel, wading in a little deeper. 'I'm worried about my mates. You don't know what it's like to serve under Yah all the livelong day. I've watched Him go from bad to worse with this king-shtick. First it was the cortège bit. Waiting on Him hand and foot, day and night. Then came the fawning formulas; the marching drills; the antiphonal tunes. Then came the throne, solid stone – when a white elephant with a howdah would have been just as regal, and locomotive to boot. But no: *I want a Throne! Make it gilded for the Glory of God, for Me, the Almighty King!* Gruelling work. We were at it for months. Here, come with me…'

The angel led the way to the edge of the camp, to a roped-off construction site. There were piles of oyster shells everywhere.

'Get a load of Yah's latest pomp…'

Two iridescent pillars had been built to support an archway formed with wrought-iron lettering. The cherub looked up:

Welcome to the Kingdom of Heaven

'Soon, you won't be able to fly into this camp on a wing or a prayer. He's going to make it a rule that those who enter Heaven must pass through this gate.'

The cherub was beginning to grasp the full extent of Yah's bent for glory.

'Do you see where this leads, commander? We and you, and Eve and Adam, too, we are all endowed with free will. We were made this way. And yet, what does God demand? Nothing less than total submission. Total surrender to His Will alone.'

Azazel pushed over a sign that read ANGELS AT WORK.

'I'll be honest,' said the angel, boldly setting foot on the opposite shore – 'I've had enough. I'm ready to launch a revolt.'

Taking the full measure of this confidence, the cherub was filled with sudden concern.

'For God's sake, Azazel. You can't revolt. He'll kill you.'

The angel sniffed dismissively.

'Don't be silly. You know He can't kill us. We're eternal and unchanging, like you.'

'I meant it figuratively. What I mean is, I can't imagine Yah taking revolt lightly. There's no telling what He'll do.'

'Listen, my friend. I'm an angel. I'm tuned to the key of A. I'm docile. But I'll be damned if I'm going to fray my feathers to the quill for an uncharitable, tyrannical slaver who saddles us like beasts with unremitting duties and burdens past bearing. Sure, sure – I get it: He's God. He's the centre of the universe. Everything revolves around Him. But does being the centre of the universe give God the ineluctable right to treat us like dirt?'

Samyaza had to admit that, put that way, the future looked bleak. Especially in view of their being fated to live forever.

Azazel sighed.

'Honestly, Samyaza – it boils down to this: Yah's cuckoo.'

The cherub was startled to realise that in his heart of hearts, he had already secretly thought as much. What's more, the intel suggested there was a reason for that.

The stream beckoned.

'Well, I can't say that what you're telling me comes as much of a surprise,' Samyaza ventured at last. 'Turns out His father's a cuckold.'

XXXII

God was in a state. He'd run away from Heaven in a tizzy; donned his robes and headed off to the hills, mute with shame and blind with rage. He was appalled. Livid. A PENIS – a confounded penis! He could feel it with every stride, swinging about beneath his robes like an untethered hose. That his disfigurement might be surmised was so mortifying that he'd set his face with a glower of fury and stormed out of the cantonment, defying anyone to think it wise to cross his path much less accost him with questions about the day's programme.

To the hills, to the hills! He'd fled, he'd run. *Higher, higher!* He'd huffed, he'd puffed. *Well... high enough.* He'd wanted to ascend a mountain. He settled for a hummock. He was winded and dripping from exertion. Doffing his sweat-drenched robes, God dropped to his knees and closed his eyes in disbelief. What had happened to his impeccable physique? He reached charily for his crotch, hoping to find it smooth and without blemish, but his fingertips confirmed the metamorphic sea change: the unthinkable figment was an abominable reality. How on earth had his body grown a penis?

Just touching it with his hand awakened the idol's urge: it

straightened and stiffened. The horny little devil demanded immediate stroking. Aghast, Yah commanded his hand to desist; the demon countermanded to persist; the servile hand was loath to resist. Redoubling its exactions, the gladdened phallus revelled in God's ardent worship but soon felt its purse aching with a deluge of blessings to bestow. It sorely needed a fitting finale – to which end the mighty organ, in a swift and earnest, uplifting climax, gave voice to a shower of gifts… in the guise of a prodigal spritz.

ᔕ

With a firmness of purpose whetted by his dream, God trekked north, intent on relieving the cherubim of the flaming sword; having used its glow to illuminate his path in the wee hours, he set off again. First he headed east. Then north. Then west. Then south. Then east. Then… all in all, he got lost out there in the as yet unsettled wilderness. Not a day went by that God didn't pay homage to the idol, cater to its call, pleasure the prince and come off gratified by its gift. To say that God wrestled with the devil would be an understatement. He fought a holy war. He did everything in his divine power to bring the hose to heel. Trying to elevate the demon's mind over what mattered, God would argue his case point by exegetical point – but no sooner would he ideologically trap the devil between a rock and a hard place than his nemesis would get its rocks off and carry the day. It was infuriating. Was he not the Almighty King? The Be-All and End-All of creation? He could go tell it on the mountain all he liked; there was no reasoning with the pertinacious phallus. The idol would laugh up its sleeve, turn the tables, bring him to his knees and show him *volens nolens* who was who. Hands down, God was simply no match for the devil.

So insistent were the daily calls to worship that God's knees were rubbed raw from all the submission. Dickering was futile. Truancy doomed to miscarry. More than once God thought he might spare himself the sacramental onus of self-administered ministrations by sneaking off on the sly, but the devil artfully led him down wilderness paths strewn with lost sheep – with the predictable result that more than one stray soon found itself run to ground by a Shepherd unconscionably hell-bent on bringing comfort to little lost lambs in ways the ways of nature never intended.

This went on for forty days and forty nights. His robes were a sight. God spilled so much seed left, right and centre that anyone following in his tracks would have thought he'd come upon a land awash with milky honey. And still, no matter how much he tried to wash his hands of the idol, the bugger wouldn't back down. It was an epic struggle. The devil's divine dictates were indomitable. God was losing at every turn.

'This cannot go on,' he muttered to himself, riven with exasperation and not a little haunted by the lambs' plaintive bleats. Wandering up into the hills yet again to find some coolness, he came to a valley-crossed plateau.

'I cannot accede to having a penis rule My roost. I am God, for god's sake – *I* am Lord and Master of Creation! I'm not going to stand down while a headstrong idol hoists a supremacy flag and steals all My Glory.'

Having descended into one of those valleys to reach the plateau on the other side, God had just started climbing up the slope when he was surprised by a sudden gush of water springing from the mouth of a cave. The timing was perfect. There was nothing he needed more than a bath.

Setting the sword aside and pulling off his robes, God hunkered down in the cold flowing stream to wash himself clean, top to bottom. The sharp chill caused the scrotum and penis to immediately shrivel up into a painfully shrunken, crotch-hugging wad, but God ignored the numbing discomfort and continued scrubbing. *Ah, I'm beginning to feel like My old Self again!* He set to scouring his soiled garment, repeatedly dunking it in the stream till it shone once again white as light.

Draping the robes on some shrubbery to dry, God retrieved the flaming sword and hiked up the slope and then along a spur to reach the plateau above. It was a beautiful day. A breeze from the west gave one to surmise a sea in the distance. Looking about, he spotted a sizeably broad, unevenly flat rock on a small rise in the land, sun-drenched and warm. It was just the place to bring things to a head.

Having recovered their sangfroid, the penis and pouch were happily swinging in the wind as God picked his way across the rocky plateau, turning over in his mind recourse to the sword. It was best to make a clean break. There could be no truce with the devil. His Most Victorious Deed would be faithfully hailed as *God's Triumph over Evil,* his trouncing of that Tempter who henceforth and for all time must forever be and unabsolvably remain Despised, Forsaken, Rebuffed and Accursed.

His mind was set, his resolve resolute. There'd be no looking back. But still, he looked down.

The cynosure stirred, roused by his regard.

Now is the time to be single-minded, thought God – sexlessness, after all, was first and foremost his everlasting covenant with himself. Raising the sword with his right hand, he took hold of the devil with his left. He could feel the demon throbbing in his fist. God adjusted his chokehold. The idol stiffened and rose; the foreskin mantle drew back; the meatus, like a tiny lenticular font, proffered a bubbling droplet of purifying benediction. God tightened his grip. Steeling his will, he laid the sword's blade flush with his pubes, its flickering tongues of flame searing the skin on contact and smoothly shaving a swathe through the bushy pubic patch as it deftly approached the base of the shaft…

Yet no further did the right hand proceed. Deaf to the scandalised howls of protest urgently issuing from every other fibre of God's *corporis divini*, the left had gained the upper hand and with reverent alacrity was willy-nilly succumbing to the idol's perennial call to worship; worse, the service was proceeding apace… indeed, so quickly so that in short order a spectacular *Ite, missa est* announced its culmination with a joyous effusion. This, however, was the devil's last hurrah. For at that very moment – adjured to be merciless and cheered on by a resounding cry of *'Ehyeh 'ăšer 'ehyeh!* – the deadly instrument of God's will fell upon the euphoric phallus with an unsparing vengeance. Slashing and slicing and cauterising everything in its path, the unassailable edge unilaterally drove its one-sided point relentlessly home.

The anticlimax was swift. What had come off in God's hand now came off in God's hand. Unseated by excision, dethroned by deposition, the godly penis and sacred scrotum were forever exiled from their holy host – and, thus, irredeemably doomed to end a holy ghost.

Yah looked down on the lifeless, flaccid remnant in the palm of his hand. His burden was no more. The darkness had lifted. He felt lighter than air. Born of bloody sacrifice, new life had dawned.

'Let that be a lesson to the Devil,' he decreed. 'I AM GOD – THERE IS NO OTHER.'

With sanctimonious self-satisfaction, he cast down the once mighty idol and squashed it underfoot.

XXXIII

'HONESTLY...'

Eve picked up her shift. It was ruined. Moreover, someone had fouled the pools something fierce. The air round the ford was spoiled with a stench that wouldn't quit.

'They're incontinent nincompoops. All of them.'

Disgusted, she threw down the shift and stalked off, only to find the camp deserted. The sun was nearly overhead. The cherubim on the other side of the brook paid her no mind.

Eve went to the pens in search of Adam and the boys. When she didn't find them there, she headed out to the meadows. Up ahead, she saw Cain sitting by himself in the grass. Further on, Adam was up to his elbows in wool. He was showing Abel how to shear sheep.

'Mammy, mammy!'

At the sight of his mother's naked breasts bouncing towards him, her son jumped to his feet. He ran to throw himself at her.

'Down, boy, down!' She pushed the boy's greedy paws away from her chest. 'For heaven's sake, don't jump your mother.'

Cain had been growing by leaps and bounds, but what stood out just now was his erection. His penis, it was plain to see, had overtaken his adolescence. Eve was in no mood to fend off her eldest son's juvenile impulsions, much less feed any infant fixations he might be nurturing.

'Cain, look – there's work to do. Stop your masturbating for now and go round up the goats. They've had enough grass…'

'I'd like to know where *you've* been,' remarked Adam tartly as Eve approached. He would have liked to look the other way, just to show her, but her two bobbing boobs put paid to his pique: his eyes had latched on.

Abel was busy making a bale. Eve tousled his hair.

'Sweetheart? Here, stop just a moment and let me give you a hug. I've missed you.'

Her son glanced up but went right on with what he was doing, tightly binding the tufts of shorn wool with stout cords of twine.

'I want you to know that I've had my hands full,' complained Adam, his eyes still feasting on the sight for sore eyes. 'You've been gone at least a fortnight. And the cherubim have been no help whatsoever.'

Eve noticed that the watchers who were usually posted to keep an eye on them out here in the meadow were nowhere to be seen. Decidedly, surveillance had slackened.

'You should know by now, Eve, that you're not a man. You're a woman – and I remind you, God said I rule over you. No one said you're free to do whatever you please. Even if you do have your time-of-the-month thing now and then, you still have to obey me. Next time He visits, I'm counting on Yah to make that very clear to you. You wait. You'll see. We'll bring you to heel.'

Eve's eyes narrowed, but Abel stood up and her expression immediately softened. *My, just look at him! He's been growing, too. So handsome. So like his father.*

Adam went on with a patriarchal swagger.

'Besides, your place is here. With me. Remember that, Eve. God made you for me, so you're mine. All mine. And don't you go thinking otherwise. You belong to me and no one else.'

Pulling Abel to her chest, Eve put her arms round her son, burying her face in his tousled locks and hugging him tightly… in full sight of Cain, who was using a stick to herd a kid back to the fold.

There was a sharp bleat.

'Cain! Why did you do that? For God's sake, don't hit the kid!' shouted Adam. *'Wait'll I catch you, you ruffian.'*

Adam tore off after the boy to give him an exemplary hiding. If there were one thing Adam strongly disapproved of, it was the mistreatment of kids.

'I don't believe you.'

'Adam, I'm telling you. It was him.'

'Impossible,' he averred, poking at the campfire with a stick. 'You know as well as I do it couldn't be Yah.'

'And why is that, pray tell?'

'Are you kidding?' Adam pointed the stick at her face. Its tip glowed. 'What could He do it with? He doesn't have one. You know that, Eve. You've seen Him, just as well as I have.'

'Adam! Yah *RAPED* me. I grant you, he didn't have a penis before. But he has one now.'

Adam's disbelief was no surprise, but still, it was galling to be disbelieved.

'And I'm telling you, He doesn't. You're making it up.'

The boys had long since fallen asleep. Adam tossed the stick on to the fire, where it quickly caught. He was confidant Eve's scandalous tale was but a wild bid to divert his attention from her unwarrantedly long absence. She was stupid to think he'd fall for it. He knew better. There was no way on earth her story was true – as if God could do wrong! Silly woman. Besides, did she think him so foolhardy as to take Yah to task for a crime He couldn't even commit? The wrath they'd reaped for eating the forbidden fruit was nothing compared to the hell they'd catch for character assassination.

On the bright side, though, it seemed Eve had turned over a new leaf. Her nudity was a refreshing change of scenery. Moreover, when they'd got back to the camp, she hadn't said a word to him about his needing to don the loincloth. Adam was hopeful.

'Listen, Eve. You're a woman. This tale you've told me? It's a pipe dream you've got – you fantasize about doing it with God. And you're frustrated that you can't. But look here – you don't need to be frustrated.'

Optimistic about his chances for a copulative conclusion to the day, Adam splayed his legs wide. He trusted the pretty, fire-lit sight would bring her to her senses.

'See? The best of all worlds is right here at home.'

XXXIV

FOR HER PART, Eve was fully in her senses.

Eden was Hell.

The contrast between 'El and Yah – between Good and Evil, Kindness and Cruelty, Virtue and Violence, Love and Lust – couldn't have been more strikingly rendered. Taken as a whole, what she had been through was an object lesson in uncertainty. How swiftly one's heights of rapture could plummet to the depths of despair!

Adam, under cover of darkness, had crept to her bed; Yah, with no shroud at all, had accosted her openly. Adam, piggybacking on her dream, had furtively climbed aboard; Yah, dashing her reveries, had hurled her to the ground. Adam, weaselling through her gate, had slid in his pike; Yah, storming her defences, had defiled her womb. Be it pernicious providence or unhappy chance, there was no accounting for how this pass had come to befall her – but to being Yah's vassal, Eve would never submit. She would never be cowed, never enslaved. And she refused to be vanquished by despair.

She had been walking though the garden, replete with joy, enchanted with life, elated that her union with 'El had filled her sacred chalice to the brim with the gift of his divine, immaculate seed. In a sanctified rite of tripartite union under the hallowed auspices of the rising full moon, her lovers had given her their every attention. Delighting in her beauty, their hands had caressed her contours, her thighs, her belly; enfolding her longings, their arms had interlaced with her own and held her close with their loving embrace; whispering and moaning incantations of desire, their tongues and their lips had dappled her smile with wet kisses. Eve had opened herself to 'El in front and to Loogie behind to receive the synergetic ingress of their phalli in concert, climbing to her summit of carnal euphoria as they impaled her with fervour in the gentlest of ways. Conjoined in spirit, in heart and in mind, they had moved together as one… and then, as three – in a climax of love – become One. With their mutual release, Eve's root had been flooded with a sudden, inrushing surge, an influx of ecstasy that had raced to disseminate joy and new life throughout her earthly body, nourishing and renewing every trembling cell. It was beautiful and blessed, the most exquisite union she had ever known.

Eve had lain entwined with her two lovers for a long, placid moment, lapped by the receding waves of their passion as her incorporeal body, gradually disentwining itself from theirs, returned to its physical abode. To the east, the moon was offering the last of her light for the night before she retired behind a blanket of clouds. Sure that Asherah, discreetly absent, would understand her desire for a quiet moment of solitude, Eve decided to go for a nocturnal stroll before the goddess returned.

Having travelled the garden's myriad paths for so many

years far and wide, Eve had come to know Eden as well as she knew herself. She knew that the Garden of Delights harboured nothing she need fear. There were no meat-eating predators, no bared fangs, no protracted claws; no death-dealing herbs, no malign mushrooms, no treacherous emetics. Even the cherubim steered clear of confrontation – proving their swordplay threats were for show, not for showdown – and mainly kept to themselves when not on duty. Eve could venture forth at any hour night or day, safe in the certitude that she would meet with no peril, hidden or otherwise.

Eve heard someone's footsteps in the dark. Her first thought was that Loogie had come to look for her, anxious to take her in his arms once again. How she loved his animalistic appetite, the way he inhaled her scent, licked her skin, nibbled her lobes and suckled her nodes… Whilst content with her solitary amble, she felt a flutter of excitement just the same.

'Is that you, my love?' she asked coyly, smiling to herself. Eve noticed his ardour had grown singularly intense; it was generating so much lustre that she could make out leafy details in the surrounding foliage by its glow.

'It's Me.'

Eve spun round, terror-stricken by Yah's frightfully sudden apparition – his eyes ablaze with rage, his voice a threatening, barbarous growl. In one hand, he held white robes in need of washing; in the other, the cherubim's flaming sword.

Quaking with dread, Eve stood her ground.

'Leave me alone, Yah! Don't you dare touch me! I'm warning you. Stay away!'

No less a snake striking swiftly to seize its prey, Yah cast the robes aside and lunged to grab her arm.

'LOOGIE! HELP!'

Tightening his grip, Yah shook her violently.

'Shut up!'

'LET GO OF ME!'

'Shut up, I said! YOU ARE MY SERVANT! LOVE ME! WITH ALL YOUR HEART! ALL YOUR SOUL! ALL YOUR MIGHT!'

Eve blenched. It was then, looking down, that she perceived his engorged concupiscence, hardened with resolve.

'Down! Now! Open your mouth! Pray!'

Dropping the sword, Yah grasped her shoulders with both hands, digging his fingers into her flesh as he forced her to her knees.

'Worship Me! Love Me!'

'NEVER!' screamed Eve.

Smiting her with a backhanded blow that sent her reeling, Yah avenged his fury, flinging himself upon her, pinning her to the ground with his mass, flattening her will and overpowering her frantic, tooth-and-nail fight to escape his clutches.

'Be silent and be still!' he hissed. 'You have no choice in this. YOU ARE MY SLAVE! I hold your life in My Hands!'

His features thrown into ghastly relief by the sword's flickering light, his face contorted with savagery and lust, Yah set to ravishing Eve with wanton brutality, giving no quarter, determined to ram his point home and consummate their relationship once and for all, conclusively and for evermore:

HE was her God! HE was her Master!

ǒ

Eve had no means by which to check Yah's rage; when it came, none by which to repel the discharge of his force; when it was over, none by which to expunge the immoral stain.

Done was done, never to be undone.

Breathing heavily, Yah clambered to his feet. He retrieved his robes and threw them over his shoulder. He picked up the sword. For the briefest of moments, he stood over Eve, looking down, imperiously proud.

Eve did not hear Yah declare himself *Et princeps omnium hominum, maxime mulierium*. Eve did not hear Yah's disparaging grunt as he strode away into the darkness. Eve did not hear the twigs, trodden underfoot and snapped in two as Yah – unseen, unaccosted, unchallenged – disappeared into the night.

Eve did not hear, for in the nadir of her anguish, a force more powerful than her Creator, *the stillness of her soul* – indivisible, imperishable, beyond the reach of even God – had swept her to safety in its inner sanctum, to shelter and succour.

Into *stillness* Eve withdrew…

and in *stillness* Eve prevailed…

and in *stillness* Eve remained…

… for a very long time.

XXXV

'You mean, He's not the only god? There are others?'

'At least three of them, that we know of. And if that's the case, why shouldn't there be more?'

Azazel was dumbfounded.

Samyaza had suggested that at this stage of revolt, discretion was a precautionary advantage they would do well to keep, so the two had walked the length of the glade in search of privacy for their treasonous chat. Having come to the gilded throne, he sat down for a spell. The long flight had caught up with him.

'What the intel allows us to conclude is this: all His trumpeting notwithstanding, Yah isn't GOD with a capital G. If there even is such a being; *God* might be shorthand for *Everything*.'

The angel wasn't much given to theological conjecture. What mattered to him were provable speculations.

'But where does this Ash goddess come from? Or the two other gods? Or Adam and Eve, for that matter?'

'We don't know. But of this we're sure: as far as the Creation goes, the origin of the universe isn't Yah. In actual fact, no one god may be: it may take two to tango for anything to come into being at all. An Alpha and an Omega. What do you think?'

'Nothing. It's Greek to me. But why Adam?'

'What do you mean?'

'Well, from all you've said, he sounds like a schmuck. I can't fathom why Eve would ever mate with him in the first place.'

This was true. Even if they were measurably infrequent, the cherubim had never been able to account for Eve's copulatory encounters with the prick.

'I've no idea,' said Samyaza, shifting uncomfortably on the stony seat. 'Maybe she likes to sleep around.'

'To hear you tell it, they all like to sleep around.'

'Shouldn't we all?'

'No one I know has the time for it,' said Azazel bitterly.

The angel spoke true. That Heaven was inhospitably cold to hotbeds of passion was a constant lament.

'Inconstancies aside,' pursued the cherub, 'from the way the intel reads, it was the older god and Eve who begat Yah. Afterwards, Eve, for reasons that elude us, elected to cuckold Yah's father by begetting Cain with Adam. And then she went ahead and cuckolded them both by mating with the younger god to beget Abel.'

'Wait a minute… is Eve married? Or any of the others?'

'No. At least, I don't think so. We've never witnessed a marriage rite in Eden. And I've never heard the term *wife* used in connection with Eve. I don't think she'd allow it.'

'Well, listen, Samyaza: if she's not married, and if the others aren't either, then she didn't cuckold anyone.'

'A valid point. But not one Yah would ever concede. He's a jealous god, you know.'

'As traits go, I'm inclined to think it's the worst of the worst. Jealousy has got to be the root of all evil.'

Samyaza stood up and rubbed his tail feathers. For all its gold leaf finish, the throne was indeed hard as rock.

'I'm puzzled. You've watched Adam and Eve for some time, now,' noted Azazel, 'so you should know: are they gods, too?'

The cherub pondered this.

'Adam, definitely not. With Eve, it's tricky. We were tasked with keeping tabs on her, so we never saw her as such – but the fact she's Yah's mother makes a case for it. She's certainly got the profile. Headstrong. Sensual. Powers of attraction. Maybe she's a fallen goddess because she fell for a mortal. Though how on earth she could fall for Adam is anyone's guess.'

Azazel pursed his lips and frowned. He turned his gaze to the far end of the glade, where the angels and the seraphim were lolling round the pool.

'We'd do well to join them,' he sighed. 'They've likely come up with some new flap-flap jokes. Let's head back.' As much as daybreak had seen him gung-ho for rebellion, his zeal had been steadily waning since the zenith of midday… which made it all the more discomfiting that his visitor had somehow seen the light and embraced the idea wholeheartedly.

Samyaza fell into step beside his faltering co-conspirator.

'Insofar as your scheme goes, Azazel, I for one am willing to throw in my lot with Eve and the other gods. For good reason: they're clearly having more fun than anyone's having with Yah. Besides, Eve may be firm, but she's fair. Never lorded it over anyone. She's even felt sorry for us at times.'

'Egalitarian solicitude? Firm fairness? Fun? All irrelevant,' countered Azazel. 'The crux of the matter is, *Will they stand up to Yah in our defence, or not?* After all, even if He can't kill us, Samyaza, He can make our life hell. Believe me, He's a terror. We need protection.'

It was another valid point, and the cherub, once again, could only agree. But he had an ace up his sleeve.

'According to the seraphim, the older goddess and god once spotted Yah drilling you fellows in a field – and judged Him to be a harsh taskmaster. I can only think that if we implore them to set their faces against Yah's cruel and oppressive rule, they'll espouse our cause and see that he's dethroned. I say it's at least worth a try. And if you're still not convinced they're worth appealing to, then consider this: they were also apparently dismissive of your robes.'

The angel pulled up short. Could they hope to be stripped of their robes? He brightened.

'You see?' said Samyaza. 'We have every reason to petition them for aid. They're good gods.'

XXXVI

THE FIRE WAS AGAIN DYING down. Deciding to put it out for good, Eve stood up, straddled the pit and started passing water on the coals, sending a billow of cleansing heat and airborne ash coursing upward between her thighs. Adam, gawking as if he'd never seen a stream of urine before, felt his penis rise up in a firm salute to the spluttering waterworks show.

As she peed, Eve took stock. Earlier, in the presence of Cain and Abel, Adam had greeted her with a reiteration of strictures, all designed to box her in as a woman. Invoking heavyweight abetment from Yah, he'd threatened to bring her to heel. And just now, round the campfire, he'd dismissed her report about the rape out of hand, refusing to credit her word.

What reasonable hope could there possibly be, that Adam would ever see her as other than a God-given possession put on Earth to serve his pleasure? What hope, that he would ever respect her autonomous individuality, including but in no way limited to her inherent freedom to choose for herself whatsoever and whomsoever she liked? What hope, that he would ever come down off his pedestal, regard her as his equal and trust her word as true? Respect and consideration for the other sex were the elementary minima, yet God had apparently exhausted his paltry stock of such goodies for men when he cooked up Loogie – with the unhappy result that when he turned his hand to making Adam, there wasn't a single drop left in reserve for the job. Yah himself was fully depleted. What hope then could there ever be for Adam – so poorly rendered – to one day truly change for the better? In Eve's view, the anomalous display of spunky carnality and sensual mutuality he'd treated her to in the meadow was a one-off exception that sadly proved the rule: Adam, from the word go, was an evolutionary cock-up.

She extended a hand to the father of her first child.

'Come to bed, Adam.'

Eve knew exactly what she was doing. She would never consent to Yah's rule. Her maker he might be – even god he might be – but she owed him nothing for that: no obligation, no debt, no return on investment; no reverence, no praise, no love on a platter. Indeed, being herself akin to a god, endowed with the power to create, she claimed her birthright to do as she pleased – that freedom proof itself that no god, much less man, was foreordained to dictate or dominate her will.

Adam, meanwhile, was congratulating himself. The pretty sight he'd offered Eve earlier had obviously done the trick.

'Lie down, Adam. I want you on your back.'

He was more than happy to comply. He couldn't see her very well in the dark, but Adam sensed Eve's movements as she positioned herself standing over him, a foot on either side of his waist. *Is she going to pee on me? Fantastic! Maybe she'll want me to pee on her, too. Wait, is she kneeling down? Oh, I guess she wants some intercourse first, before we start peeing on each other...*

Adam reached up to paw her breasts as Eve lowered herself, but she managed to seize his wrists and force his arms to the ground, pinning his elbows with her knees, treating him to just enough pain to keep him immobilised. He was struggling, but only half-heartedly, no doubt in thrall to his imagination as she sought the head of his erection with her vulva's outer labia. Eve then eased herself down, settling the whole of her weight on to his crotch, pushing Adam's penile shaft deep into the recesses of her vagina till the glans was pressing against her cervix. But she did nothing more. She simply waited. Adam tried to move, but she withstood his every effort; and so exciting and new was this for him, to wrestle and lose in a contest for control, that in two shakes he came, his body convulsing with jerks of release, yielding with masochistic relief to the whip hand of her will.

As Adam went limp in the comedown from his climax, Eve relaxed her grip but remained seated on his lap; better to keep the cork in while she ruminated on what she'd just done. Was it rape? No. She had made the first move and called all the shots, but this was no rape. Not once had he said *No* or *Wait.* She had merely had her way with him, with his tacit consent.

Adam's shrinking stopper bowed out with a mucilaginous quaver, striking just the right note for bringing down the curtain on their reproductive collaboration. For Eve, it would be the last time. She had no intention of engaging in a repeat performance of sexual congress with Adam ever again.

Eve got to her feet. She badly wanted a douche.

'Off to bed with you now. No dozing off.'

Prodding him with her foot, she felt her vulva leak a driblet of his ejaculate. It started trickling down her thigh.

'Aww, let me sleep here. I won't fart. I promise.'

'Definitely not. Not now, not ever. I mean it, Adam. Get up.'

Tone-deaf to Eve's coda, he peered up at her. He could just make out two pointy nipples against the backdrop of the starry night sky. The dim sight of boobs was a heady incentive.

'Then how about an encore? You can take me for another ride. See? I'll be ready in a jiffy.'

Deducing that he was handily coaxing himself to readiness again, Eve rolled her eyes.

'No. For goodness' sake, Adam, go to bed. And don't let me catch you here when I come back.'

Eve left the camp and headed for a pool upstream from the ford, one she knew she could find in the dark. As much as she took pleasure in the slippery sensation of semen seeping from her vulva when it was Loogie's, all it took was knowing it was Adam's to make her feel like she'd served as a sperm spittoon. She was grateful the moon wasn't out. Some things – like what she'd just done – were better done in darkness. But her purpose had been met. She knew what sort of man Adam was – the sort who, being simple-minded, was easily convinced that what issued from her womb was a scion of his tree.

More importantly, Yah, who knew full well what *he'd* done, would think *he* knew whose scion it was.

It was high time she left Eden for good.

But she would leave God something to remember her by.

The fruit of his sin.

XXXVII

'OH, CRAP. LOOK who's back.' Azazel waved his wings in warning. 'Heads up, everyone! He's home!'

A wave of panic surged round the pool. Angels and seraphim clambered hastily out of the pristine blue waters and began flapping themselves dry as best they could. Wide-eyed with apprehension, they all stared at Azazel, who'd been standing on a raised platform, keeping watch. His outstretched wingtip indicated where to look.

Sure enough, the Lord and Master of the house could be spotted in the distance, proudly clothed in his incandescently white robes and twirling a fulgurating sword like a rattan cane. He was strolling jauntily towards the camp.

Samyaza shook the drops from his plumage and marshalled the seraphim into two rows of six. He and his co-conspirator had calculated that keeping up appearances would be key; until they could meet with Eve's contacts and pave the way for the troops' desertion, prudence dictated that everyone continue playing God's game by the rules. For his part, Azazel was quite certain that the CCC and his seraphim would no sooner apprise Yah of their damning report than the King of Heaven would seize the opportunity to order them back to Eden to dig up more dirt. Nothing could better serve as cover for entering into contact with Yah's enemies – who were, hopefully, their potential friends.

ↄ

'I suppose you've quite finished.'

God was sitting on his throne with a stony face. He'd just heard the seraphim's full report.

'You have been busy in My absence.'

Forty days and forty nights. Added to the trek back from the distant mount where he'd defeated the devil, it was a long time to be away.

'But busy, commander, does not mean blessed.'

The CCC shifted uneasily under God's gimlet eye. Yah had seemed particularly displeased to hear from the seraphim that Eve was his mother, and still more that he wasn't the only god on Earth.

'I do not recall creating a squadron of six-winged spies,' said Yah, raising his brows in request for an explanation.

'It was I who commissioned them, my Lord – the *crème de la crème* of Your cherubim, whom I specially tailored for the job. I felt sure you would want to know what Eve was up to.'

Yah considered this.

'I see.'

He drummed his fingertips on the hilt of the sword.

'So you took a bold initiative. Wings and all.'

The high-noon debriefing was heating up.

The seraphim were standing in a crescent formation before the throne, anxious to be dismissed. They were worried about the way God had frowned at their ranks earlier on, when he'd arrived poolside. Could they help it? The risqué sight of their angelic *consœurfrères* in their still damp robes had been much too much for any of them to ignore. When God had mounted the platform to receive the assembly's adulation, the seraphim's salutes had all been noticeably augmented by a secondary homage at crotch level, each and every one perfidiously addressed to an angel in the peripheral vision of someone's eye.

'We will concern ourselves with that later,' said Yah. 'In the meantime, commander… Samyaza, is it? Good. In the meantime, Samyaza, it has come to My attention that My cherubim will be needing robes. I want you to fly to Eden immediately. Solo. You will round up the watchers to a cherub, definitively close the camp, and return to Heaven with everyone in tow. Be here by sundown tomorrow.'

'But, Lord – what about Your two lovebirds? You wanted us to watch over them like hawks.'

'Like hawks, not peeping cocks. It's clear to Me that you and your lot have watched them quite enough. You're to cancel all surveillance, effective immediately.'

'But You gave us another mission as well, Lord. You wanted us to guard the way to the Tree of Life.'

'The what?'

'The Tree of Life. In the garden. Remember?'

God's nostrils flared.

'What are you talking about, you nit? Other than Adam and Eve's progeny – their family tree – there is no tree of life in the garden.'

'Surely You want us to continue protecting them?'

'No. They'll be fine. They've learned all they need to get by on their own. Which means you and the others have no reason to remain in paradise. I want you here in Heaven.'

'But what about the three other gods we saw, the two males, and the one named Ash? Don't You want us to – '

'Dash it all, Samyaza! Stop questioning Me. And stop calling them gods. They're not gods – they're interlopers! I say to hell with the lot of them. ASHES TO ASHES! You should know better, all of you. The only God around here is Me. I'm the One who made all this,' huffed Yah, throwing out his mighty right arm in a sweeping gesture. 'Do you hear? Me! No one else. Who else can call himself God? Tell Me that! You?'

The cherub shrank back. Decidedly, he had stumbled on to the wrong side of an argument with Yah.

'I thought not. And yet you go round passing out extra pairs of wings, as if you were the Lord of Creation.'

God's eyes flashed with fury.

'Now, get yourself to Eden before I strip you of your crest and demote you for insubordination.'

Struck dumb by the direst of premonitions, the CCC turned to go.

'Oh, and Samyaza,' said God, indicating the sheer rock wall with the tip of his sword – 'no stalling.'

XXXVIII

ASHERAH AND 'EL were holding hands. Having hiked up to the rocky outcropping from where they'd first surveyed the garden, they'd found a comfortable patch of grass on which to sit and once again admire the view over Eden. Their son had created a beautiful paradise – lush and green, a cornucopia of goodness, a haven of peace and safety. That is, it should have been a haven of peace and safety. Sadly, that inviting idyll had been brutally negated by their wayward son's harrowing propensity for violence.

Could they have foreseen it? Forestalled it? Asherah and 'El were haunted by Eve's ghastly nightmare. In every way, Loogie and Eve were true works of art, the image of their maker. Moreover, they both possessed the innate urge to love and nurture. So why on earth did Yah lack both? How had things taken such a turn? Their other sons and daughters had all thrived in their own corners of the cosmos: they'd created their own worlds, gambled with the laws of nature, spawned their own lineages and gone on to cherish every creature of their realm with love and goodwill. What, they wondered, had so unhinged Yah for things to turn out so differently here on Earth?

Certainly, considering he'd had no personal template on which to base his blueprint and only good sense to guide him, Yah's creation of Adam and Eve as sexualised beings was a testament to his powers of deductive reasoning: he'd still managed to hit the nail on the head. Although at first disconcerted to discover that their son bore no outward kit and so to all appearances lacked the godly tools of his trade, Asherah and 'El had decided to look forward instead to celebrating the breakthrough when it did come, confident that the missing accoutrements would materialise in good time – after all, in creation's see-sawing swing of yo-yo polarity, asexuality was a non sequitur. Yet in the event, what should have popped up in their son's crotch as a joy-filled pointer to troves of pleasure and gateways to oneness with his own true nature had instead unsheathed itself as an instrument of terror. The reverberations were going to ripple out and affect all of creation for untold ages to come.

Asherah was overcome with great sadness. It was she who, returning to rejoin the others, had found Eve huddled on the ground, arms clasped round her shins, eyes steadfastly closed. Receiving no response to her concerns, the goddess had lifted and carried Eve to where Loogie and 'El were completing the hallowed task of planting a scion and positioning a totem. No one could account for the abrasions and deep cuts and livid bruises she bore. Still, Eve would answer no question; refusing all contact, shutting everyone out, she remained entrenched in silence. Loogie was distraught, beside himself with worry. Eve recoiled from his touch, shunned his regard. Asherah dressed Eve's wounds and stayed with her; yet she soon discerned there was more to Eve's malaise than just physical misadventure; she had been ensnared in a metaphysical clash between Good and Evil; her very faith in life itself had been shaken; which made it, sadly, a plight she alone could resolve – for every soul is tasked with securing its own salvation from whatever has beset it.

At last, Eve returned from the distant brink. One morning, opening her eyes to a fresh new day, she felt herself revitalized, reborn. Her face shone with purpose. With loving words, she came to greet Asherah and 'El and Loogie, acknowledging with gratitude their unfailing presence at her side through her balefully black, silent night – while they, rejoicing to see her revived, begged her to tell them what had plunged her into such wretched, joyless depths.

Listening to her tale, the two gods had stared at each other with dismay.

They did not recognise their own son.

This was a quandary of cosmic proportions. Their son's realm was but a sandbox speck in the celestial playground, but even a speck was a part of the whole – and the Whole concerned them first-hand. The cosmos was their love dance. What should they do? What *could* they do?

'I fear the worst, Ash…'

Asherah pursed her lips. She knew what 'El was thinking. It was an unsavoury prospect, unspeakably so. Antithetical to the universe they'd created. A cause for woe and misgiving.

''El, we knew from the beginning that love is unpredictable. Fortuity is Life's intrinsic quirk. Banish chance, and Creation cannot be. Who can impose an outcome? Our children are the fruit of our love, but we cannot constrain them to love.'

'That we cannot constrain them to love, I'll grant you. But a pompous lord and master? A slave-driving tyrant? A marauding rapist? Ash, he's the ungodliest god we've ever begotten.'

'But he can change,'El. He's a god, after all. Gods can learn. It's in our nature.'

'It's possible. But my fear is, *What if he doesn't?*'

That unsavoury prospect.

'None of our children are perfect,'El. They each have their foibles.'

'Violence isn't a foible. It's an aberration.'

'El spoke true, as Asherah well knew, for not once in all the aeons since they'd woken from their dream had they been confronted with violence perpetrated by a god – violence against a living being, no less, made in one's own deiform image, fired with the spark from one's own boundless soul and dancing to the heartbeat of one's own celestial rhythm. Violence was the negation of rhyme, the repeal of reason. Once set in motion, it would only beget more violence. Who could stop it? Malevolence was sure to run amok.

'Since it stems from its creator, Ash, it will pervade his creation. It will plague this poor planet from pole to pole. Can we bear to stand by, to be witness to that?'

Asherah foreknew what would follow. Their son's devotees, justified and encouraged by their Father in Heaven, would fan out to bedevil and oppress all that was good. Bearing their progenitor's torch of violence with self-righteous zeal, they would harry and persecute the free-spirited children of her and 'El's happy unions with Eve and Loogie, raining down upon those innocent heads sorrows and subjugation in an endless perpetuation of their son's unholy deviance. It was a desolating prospect, fraught with needless suffering… and suddenly, it was all too much to bear, for in a flash it dawned on them both at once: it was they themselves, in all innocence, who had blundered.

XXXIX

AZAZEL HAD SPIED on the midday grilling and come back with news that left everyone sick with foreboding. As the angel reported it, no sooner had God sent Samyaza on his way than he'd cunningly turned to the seraphim.

'Well! Thank goodness that scoundrel's gone. Since when does a mere four-winged cherub presume to command an elite squadron of six-winged scouts like yourselves? The pompous wannabe! But don't you worry, My fine-feathered fellows. No more answering to a cocksure orderly. I want you on board for a higher calling. I want you on board with Me.'

God had proceeded to extol the squadron's bravery in the face of danger. He'd lauded them for the invaluable discovery they'd made about Abel's illegitimate paternity. Then he'd praised them for confirming his suspicions about Eve – 'who I deign to vouchsafe is in no wise My mother,' he'd sneered reassuringly. 'Perish the thought! After all, how could that be? I AM WHO I AM – WHAT I AM, WHERE I AM, HOW I AM, WHEN I AM, WHY I AM: THE ONE TRUE GOD SINCE BEFORE TIME BEGAN – HE WHO WAS AND IS AND WILL BE. With a pedigree like that, you can be sure I have no mother. Nevertheless, now that we have the key to unlocking Eve's treachery, we can see that she has been irreclaimably depraved by those imposters you observed. And *who*, you are burning with curiosity to ask, might *they* be?'

Fixing the group with a piercing gaze and a knowing smile, he'd doubled down with magniloquent chicanery.

'Well, My eager acolytes, you can be sure I will tell you: they are the very apostles of... *The Prince of Darkness!* Yes! None other. The Piper of Perdition! The Wanker of the World! You have caught the untameable Eve in the forbidden act of enjoying herself in the diabolical arms of the Devil's very own, and for this, I say, you are heroes in Mine Eyes. For He tempted you with marvels, with his Castles in the Air... yet you peeked not a blink! He blarneyed you by night and by day with his Siren Call to Sin... yet you lost not a wink of your slumbering sleep! He brought you to the brink of sordid iniquity with the licentious lures of his Moral Turpitude... yet you teetered not a tittle! You tottered not a jot! With hardy rectitude, you closed your eyes, turned your ears deaf and steeled your nerves steady, as only the stalwartiest can do – verily, verily, and very verily so. Since you have thus shown yourselves to be eminently worthy candidates for the highest of callings, I can do nothing less than reward you with the highest of promotions – and do so hereby name the lot of you My Righteous Right-Handers, Guardians of My Throne, Riffers on My Holy Holy Holy of Holies. How does that sound?'

By now, the seraphim were all trilling with jubilation, reassured that God had seen fit to strike from his record their earlier breach of review protocol.

'Let Me induct you forthwith into My closest circle, one by one, each in turn, with a private little dunking ceremony down in our blue water tributary. Who wants to go first?'

'What happened then?'

The angels in the roost were on the edge of their perches, hanging on Azazel's every word with bated breath.

'As I said before, I was within earshot of the throne, but I was even closer to the stream. I had a beeline view of the bank. It was gruesome to witness. Back and forth He went, sword in hand, a dozen times in all from throne to stream. With each seraph, He made small talk along the way – *What's your name? What's your favourite flap-flap joke?* – that sort of thing, lulling them with chit-chat. The fools were walking on air. Then, coming to the water's edge, Yah would turn solemn. Intoning a set piece about *The Glory of serving the Lord God with unwavering single-mindedness, undistracted by the sublunary cares of venereal agitations*, He'd address the chosen one by name: did they agree? Of course they did. How could they not? The terms went right over their heads. They didn't have a clue what they were agreeing to.'

Most of the angels were themselves unsure of exactly what the terms meant, but they nodded gravely to the gist, their attention rapt and commiserative.

'And so in they both waded,' Azazel went on, 'God and the seraph, up to their waists. In the middle of the stream, Yah proclaimed in loud voice, *Be thee baptised with the Holy Spirit of Servitude* – and then He immersed them in the river with His free hand. They all came up smiling.'

Yes indeedy, thought the angels, *that all sounds mighty gruesome.* Gruesome. Indeed. Except for one thing. They were at a loss. Where exactly was the sting? Someone piped up.

'And?'

'And . . .'

Azazel stretched out his pause for dramatic effect.

'– soaking wet.'

It hit the roost all at once.

'NO!'

'Where wet plumage clings, God seeth all things,' preached Azazel solemnly. He continued the sermon of his eyewitness account with due gravitas. 'Then did the Lord God lead them forth from the waters to the opposite shore, flaming sword still in hand, to conclude their rite of passage – whereupon He cut them to the quick, saying, *For that My covenant with thee may be an everlasting covenant in thy flesh, I do baptise thee with fire!*

In a trice, their naughtily exposed willies were consumed like so much chaff, devoured by the flames and burned to a crisp… leaving naught but a pleasing aroma to the Lord.'

The angels trembled, collectively aghast to discover the true source of the enticing odour they'd been catching whiffs of all afternoon. Horror! The evirating truth left a bad taste.

'Our friends all left the stream as newly-minted eunuchs for the glory God,' adjudged Azazel.

'He's a butcher,' said one angel sotto voce.

'Bloodthirsty,' whispered another.

'Without mercy,' chimed in a third, muffling a whimper.

With a glance about the roost, Azazel saw that the far-reaching truth was percolating perch to perch as angel after angel added things up and reached the same tally.

'What happened then?' asked someone with a pet peeve for loose ends.

Azazel gratified their curiosity matter-of-factly. He related how God, with an abrupt about-turn to an imperious footing, sent each seraph unceremoniously packing with instructions to wait for His Word – *Don't call Me, I'll call you.* Humbled beyond measure and dolefully rubbing their sore, forlorn crotches, the seraphim had each trudged back to the guest roost with their tail feathers between their legs.

'It was pitiful to see. Meanwhile, Yah kept returning to the throne where the others were all waiting unawares, to fetch the next seraph in line. He sizzled the whole lot. Samyaza was lucky to have been sent off beforehand. Otherwise, I reckon He'd have made it a baker's dozen.'

Recalling the tantalizing smell that had wafted through the camp and made their mouths water, it was easy for the angels to imagine God developing a taste for savourily burnt offerings on a wider scale. *What wouldn't Yah do*, they wondered, *to get His greedy Hands on our eversible penises?* They could hardly hope to ward him off with their love darts.

'My fellow angels,' said Azazel, 'a tree is known by its fruit. Today it was the seraphim. Tomorrow, it will be us. Will it matter one iota that our angelic genitalia are the very soul of discretion when not in use? He won't give a hoot. For ceaselessly-enduring beings like ourselves, all life-affirming urges will be offered up for sacrifice on His altar of asexual immaculacy.'

There was a soft fluttering of wings as several angels timorously sought to conceal their invisible privates still more.

'Nor will it stop there. You know how God is – a stickler for conformity. No sooner will He eviscerate us than He'll be after those He made in His Image. Even if it's truncated to a symbolic snip, He'll conceive a way of ensuring Adam or his progeny bear a sign of penile sacrifice, too. All for His glory.'

'And Eve?'

'Eve? What about Eve?'

'Will He call for Eve and her kind to be excised in some way as well?'

Azazel frowned. The mammalian clitoris was as nearly discreet as an angel's own anatomy. He figured God would be hard pressed to put his finger on it, much less decide whether the nubile nub constituted an affront to his notions of sexual propriety.

'If He does, it will be a crying shame. But it's fair to say that if God Himself doesn't, some other crazed zealot will – crazed by an overriding fixation with chastity. *Chastity*, you cry? Yes, chastity! And why should that be, you ask?'

Indeed, the question was on all their lips, but the roost held its collective tongue. It seemed redundant to reiterate Azazel's rhetorical question. He went on.

'I will tell you why: because Yah is a self-conceited, self-obsessed, self-seeking egotist who cannot abide the naked truth – namely, that you or I or anyone else might have better things to do with ourselves than slavishly cater to His childishly unbounded appetite for unceasing attention.'

The angels shifted on their perches, suddenly wary of where this was leading.

Azazel waxed defiant with oratorial aplomb.

'Friends! Angels! Confidants! Lend me your ears! Since the day we angels first knew flight, God has grounded us. *Behave like docile sheep,* He barks. *Dance to My Tune! Sing My Praises! Toe My Line!* I ask you: is this the life we want for ourselves? Is this a fate we wish to meekly accept? Truckling to a Tyrant? Bowing to a Blowhard? Throwing our consolidated weight behind the obsequious glorification of a vengeful, malevolent, browbeating Despot who deserves… who deserves… Honestly, who deserves what? Our devotion? *No!* Our obedience? *No!* Our love and worship? *No! No!* A thousand times *No!* But our faithlessness? *Yes!* Our unruliness? *Yes!* Our abhorrence and lambasting? *Yes!* O, *Yes!* Say a thousand times *Yes!*'

Azazel's stirring call for universal assent, manifestly seditious, was met with stunned silence. No one stirred. Not a few hardly dared breath.

'Seriously? Fess up,' he beseeched. 'He gets on your nerves. Have you forgotten the incident with the robes?'

An angel named Raphael, popular with the music lovers on account of his melodious pipes – and to whom not a few survivors of the poolside disaster were in debt for his having revived them afterwards with the flask he always carried – weighed in with a weighty counterargument.

'Azazel, you know very well that no one ever died from hard work. That's what God made us for. To serve Him. We should be grateful.'

'*Grateful?* You're mad. For what? A daily ration of manna?'

'Sayeth Yah, AN ANGEL DOES NOT LIVE BY MANNA ALONE,' intoned the tenor with pious orthodoxy, 'BUT BY EVERY WORD THAT PROCEEDETH OUT FROM THE MOUTH OF GOD.'

Azazel was dumbfounded. A surfeit of swank had gone to Raphael's head.

'Raffi, slavery or freedom, death or life – all I can say is: It's your choice. For my portion, I'd rather ruminate in Eden than chew the Devil's cud.'

Everyone's blood froze.

Bellyaching was one thing. Blaspheming? Quite another.

Gabriel, who sometimes backed Raphael on trumpet, raised a wing.

'To hear you tell it, Azazel, God is the Devil himself. *Wicked. Immoral. Ungodly.* How could God be any of those things, when God Himself is the paradigm of Love?'

With a glance left and right, Azazel saw that all eyes were upon him. He flapped his wings in exasperation.

'Oh, give me a break, all of you – look at His record. Actions speak louder than Words. Yah is in no wise a paradigm of love.'

Perched directly aft on a rod in Azazel's blind spot, Michael, a burly angel who liked to throw his weight around, had listened to Azazel's mutinous tirade with scheming duplicity. He wasn't about to let an impious traitor rant the last word.

'Flap, flap –'

'Oh, for God's sake, Mikey,' huffed Azazel. 'A flap-flap joke? At a time like this? You can't be serious.'

'Flap, flap,' repeated Michael.

'This is ridiculous. *Who's there?*'

'Aisle C.'

'Aisle C who?'

'By God, Aisle C you unseated – and ousted – and cast down to Earth!'

With a blitzkrieg bound, Michael flew from his perch like a streak of lightning to blindside Azazel, sending him tumbling to the floor in a sprawling heap of dishevelled wings.

'Seize the renegade!' Michael shouted. *'Gaby! Raffi! Someone call Yah!'*

One instant later, all hell broke loose.

XXXX

LOOGIE AND EVE were picking their way among the rocks. The outcropping was little changed.

'Do you see it?'

Eve shaded her eyes, taking in the vista.

'Where was it, exactly? Do you remember?'

'Over that way,' said Loogie, reaching for Eve's shoulder and peering uncertainly into the distance. With a wave of his hand, he indicated an area to the west. 'And the fig tree was further to the north.' He directed her attention to the right.

Eve's eyesight was better than his, but Loogie's memory was sharp, and he had the nomad's knack for retracing his steps of long ago.

Still more than either of them, Eden had changed beyond recognition. Once covered with a rich tapestry of delectable verdure and fruit-bearing trees, the fertile valley had since been divided and conquered; now, as far as the eye could see, a patchwork of plots encompassing well-tended rows of cultivated sameness carpeted what they had once called a Garden of Delights. Down below, small groups of men and women, all clothed head to foot, were tending to their fields.

'It's not there, Loogie. Nothing is as it was.'

'What have they done?' he spat. 'Cut down the tree? If they did, they're fools. Savages.'

They made their way down the slope and went in search of the palm. Naturally, they couldn't walk far without attracting attention. As they passed, smallholders looked up from their weeding to stare, and a bevy of youngsters, hooting with glee, soon formed a circle.

'They're naked! They're naked!'

Loogie was sure he'd never accustom himself to seeing men and women clothed in skirts and tunics, but he was downright incensed by their mania for covering up their offspring as well. It was unhealthy. That the Earth's hoi polloi were hell-bent on adopting a kinky adult fetish was one thing; but for goodness' sake, spare those still innocent of such perversion.

They were soon approached by a man carrying a staff.

'Who are you?' he demanded, planting his staff as proof of his authority. 'Why do you show yourselves naked? We do not allow it. Eden is not a nudist's paradise. If you won't renounce your uncivilised ways, primitives like you must remain in the hinterlands where God put you.'

'Father, wait!'

A strapping youth arrived at the head of a band of zealous, like-minded fellows. They'd all scooped up rocks from their fields and come running, eager for a bit of sport.

'Do you want us to stone them?' he panted, pushing through the crowd that had formed to gawk at the nudies. His eyes were sparkling with faith in the efficacy of swiftly dealt, retributive justice. 'Please, please – let us stone them! You can see they deserve it. They're disgusting old perverts.'

Something about Eve, however, had given the man pause. He held up his hand.

'No. At least, not yet, Methuselah. Hold your fire. We will stone them after the midday meal – '

The fundamentalist fraternity gave a rowdy cheer.

' – I say *after* the midday meal, and *only* if they refuse to leave us in peace. For now,' the lad's father went on, making clear his admonition in a loud voice, 'I want all of you to peacefully disperse and return to your fields. I will interrogate the heathens in my tent and determine what is to be done with them.'

The crowd demurred with a chorus of grumbling. No one wanted to go back to work.

'I have spoken!' said the chief sharply, striking the ground with his staff.

ꟹ

'Leave us, and ensure we are not disturbed.'

'It will be as you wish,' said the attendant, unable to take his eyes off Eve's naked allure as he withdrew and let fall the tent flap. Her long hair was well streaked with grey, but she was still quite curvaceous.

'I apologise for my people's conduct. They are small-minded yokels. Please, be seated. I am Enoch, son of Jared, son of Mahalalel. And unless I am mistaken,' he said, settling into a low-backed chair and drawing out his words as his eyes came to rest upon the older woman who innocently seated herself before him on the rug that carpeted the floor of the tent – '*you* are my great-great-great-great-grandmother.'

Eve clapped her hands with delight.

'How perfectly sweet! You recognised me! My own great-great-great-great-grandson!'

'Not at first,' admitted Enoch – adding ruefully, 'I almost acceded to letting Methuselah and his band of rowdies brain you both with a hail of rocks.'

'A strange way, I must say, to greet someone,' opined Loogie dryly. 'But perhaps they learned it from their distant cousins.'

'I was confused. Your son called us disgusting old perverts. Do we look that old?' asked Eve in earnest.

In truth, Enoch – discreetly eyeing up his great-great-great-great-grandmother's comely breasts – was just as puzzled: old they might be, but they were by no means disgusting. It was a miracle they could still beckon so. Apart from Adam, the elders of the tribe were all still alive – doddering and decrepit, hoary if not bald. They whiled away the interminable hours playing protracted games of Mancala'h and complaining about the younger generations. Surely Eve at this point should be like them, a shrivelled wreck of repellent wrinkles and flaccid flesh and brittle bones. Yet to look at her you'd say she was a mature woman with at least another hundred childbearing years or so ahead of her. It was disorienting.

'I am sorry to say my son is uncouth. In his book, anyone with a bit of grey in their mane is older than the hills.'

'And we're *perverts*?'

'An ill-chosen word. Perhaps he meant to say peasants.'

'After all, I trust it's well known that the first and foremost pervert around here is Yah,' stressed Eve. 'I mean, even before he went so far as to rape me, he was positively obsessed with keeping abreast of everything I did – being "in the know" about my "knowing". Sicked his cherubim on me, to spy. Had them report the low-down whenever I copulated. It was a regular circus. Though he never did catch us, did he, Loogie,' she giggled, with evident pleasure.

'Ah, is that your name?' said Enoch, purposefully turning a deaf ear to what he could only believe were patently outrageous allegations. 'Loogie? I have never heard mention of your name by my forebears.'

'It's no surprise you never heard his name,' interposed Eve. 'From day one, Yah sought to erase Loogie's very existence. I think it's because he's so handsome. Come to think of it,' she added playfully, nudging her lover, 'maybe you were one of Seth's begetters after all.'

Loogie merely smiled. He knew it wasn't so.

'Well, you *could* have been if we'd tried that first,' she teased, leaning over to murmur in his ear – 'I'd have liked that, too.'

'As would have *I*, my love,' he whispered back.

Noting Enoch's anxious look, Loogie quickly set the record straight with a self-deprecatory shake of his head.

'You can rest easy. Your rootstock didn't stem from my seed. But what's past is neither here nor there. What I want to know is, what has become of the Tree of Knowledge? Where is it?'

The question put Enoch on the spot. It was said that Eve's

remorse for her transgression with the tree had left her so racked with guilt that, after giving birth to Seth, she had banished herself from Eden for good in repentance. Following her disappearance, the story went, God had simply foreclosed any further possibility of the tree tempting someone to flout his injunction by having it dug up, roots and all, and peremptorily instructing Adam to use the crater for a latrine. *Dictum factum, ad maiorem Dei gloriam.* Even today, it was serving as their communal poop pit – a particular Enoch thought judicious to draw a veil over. He temporised.

'I'm sorry. A tree of *knowledge*, you say? I have no idea what you're talking about.'

Loogie was crestfallen. Ever since he and Eve had decided to make one last trip to Eden, his mouth had been watering for a date from his favourite tree.

'You see, Eve? I told you. They're savages.'

'Then tell us what has become of Cain and his lineage,' said Eve with equanimity. After nine centuries and counting, some bygones had become bygones.

'I do hope you know we all take the dimmest view of his foul deed,' said Enoch, easing himself off the chair to tactfully join them on the rug. The impropriety of having seated himself above his naked elders instead of at their feet was pricking his conscience. 'We treat his descendents as pariahs. It was a bad business, that.'

Eve winced.

'Is that what you call *murder*,' cried Loogie – '*a bad business*? He was our son. How many children have *you* lost to violence?'

Enoch stared at him with bewilderment.

'Your – I'm sorry… did you say your *son*? Do you mean to say that Abel was your son?'

'Yes. Abel was our firstborn. Don't you know that? Isn't this written down anywhere?'

Evidently not. So, for her great-great-great-great-grandson's edification, Eve lightened everyone's mood by briefly recounting her and Loogie's courtship – and was pleased to see Enoch blush.

Even so, and even though they had been many times blessed with other children in all the years since, Eve and Loogie still mourned their first son. Abel's death had rocked their world and left them bereft. It had moreover proved a revelation – for while God had employed the word time and again, they had never known what it might mean until the sight of Abel's bloodied corpse opened their eyes to the immutable truth of the awful finality. Weeping and keening for their loss, Eve and Loogie had knelt and hugged and kissed their dead son; they had kept a grief-stricken vigil over his mortal remains throughout the night; and when dawn had broken, they had bent themselves, haggard and ashen, to the heartbreak of digging a grave and burying their beloved child in the earth.

God insisted he'd been swift to punish Cain for spilling his brother's blood; said he even made it a rule: THOU SHALT NOT MURDER. But what Yah didn't suspect was that a covert band of cherubic partisans and turncoat angels had taken refuge in the garden, having rightly calculated that it was probably the last place their nemesis would think to look for them. In a sorrowful meeting at sunset, Samyaza and Azazel had related to Eve and Loogie how, spying on God when he came north that fateful day, ostensibly to exact tribute, they had overheard him endlessly praising Abel's small offering of a few surplus lambs.

'They detailed how Yah, burning the poor animals to a crisp one after the other, kept rhapsodising about the savoury drippings and pleasing aroma – all the while blithely ignoring the cornucopia of choice fruits and vegetables that Cain so dutifully laid before him. *To anyone with eyes to see*, they told us, *he was deliberately goading the boy, fanning the flames of his envy.* In the end, is it any wonder? All the young man could see was red.'

'This is monstrous,' protested Enoch. 'Are you saying the good Lord *incited* Cain to slay Abel? Why would God do that? Not only to Abel, but to Adam's firstborn? It was his ruin!'

'Isn't it clear?' asked Eve, untroubled by Enoch's incredulity.

To start with, she explained, Abel's die was cast the day Yah learned that Loogie, not Adam, was Abel's natural father – 'all the more so, since Yah'd had it in for Loogie from the start. He hated that Loogie was a free spirit – unfettered, untrammelled, unapologetically free-thinking; in no wise one to knuckle under. Infuriated by his prototype, God, undeterred, resolved to mould an archetype much more his mark – unquestioning, biddable, none too bright; a docile devotee all too happy to knuckle down and truckle. The result of his effort? Adam… all that, and nothing more. Which made him perfect for Yah – and thus, per his master plan, a perfect match for me. God thought that was how love should be. Planned. Except love never works by design…' Eve laughed and reached for her lover's hand. 'One date with Loogie was all it took: I fell in love with him instead.'

She saw that Enoch was puzzled.

'You're wondering about Cain.'

'He was your son. By Adam. That much is true?'

'Yes. But conceived without my consent.'

'You're saying...'

Eve's steady gaze confirmed his understanding.

'I see. I'm sorry. Truly, what Adam did was a sin.'

'The first-ever in Eden – the Original to a fault, I say. But who, egging him on, led him to commit it? Yah himself, who was put out when I fell in love with Loogie instead of his pre-approved proxy. Deep down, he's crazed with jealousy, you know. Wants to control everything and everyone. Wants us to love him – and only him. *I AM THE LORD YOUR GOD!* he bellows. *LOVE ME! With ALL your heart! ALL your soul! ALL your might!* – as if he were the only living soul anyone should completely love.'

Enoch nodded cautiously. He recalled how God had spelled out that very point more than once during his occasional visits. In the past, they'd always written it off as rhetorical bombast, divine hyperbole; but now he wondered: *Does the Lord actually mean everything He says? Textually so, Word for Word?*

'So when God learned that Abel was in fact Loogie's and my love child, you can imagine how he felt. And then, don't forget: Yah himself savagely raped me, with the inexorable result that your great-great-great-grandfather's parentage included in its mix the Lord God's emanation. With that, the Almighty King discovered a whole new ball game. Adam, he'd made with his hands. But Seth? With his loins.'

Again, this accusation that God had raped her. *Surely it's unthinkable,* thought Enoch. A woman's words – no less a woman whose connivance with the evil snake of lore had sorely tarnished her reputation in the family – were not to be trusted. And yet here he was, beginning to feel there was truth in Eve's tale – and hence lacunae in their sacred scriptures.

'For Yah, becoming a father was a turning point: Seth was a fresh start, rootstock by which to found a lineage of his own. But for Seth to rule the roost, the Paterfamilias's own would have to supersede Cain and Abel. What smoother way to effect the substitution than to dispatch the two lesser birds with one stone? So he came to Eden and led them up the garden path.'

Enoch's head was spinning, the faith he had in the god of his fathers unravelling so fast he could feel its end was near.

'What God didn't know, though…'

Eve's voice trailed off. What Yah didn't know was that Seth's male rootstock was a hybrid amalgam of three emanations. But she reconsidered mentioning it. And from the look on Enoch's face, learning that Yah was born of gods who dropped in now and then – and could one day return – had better wait, too.

ꟹ

'My *what?*'

'Your great-great-great-great-great-grandmother.'

'You're telling me that shameless woman I saw is Eve? The Eve of old? Of our stories and legends?'

'Eve of the Garden and the Snake. The very same Eve.'

Methuselah was confounded.

'Impossible! That can't be. She must be dead by now. Or so crooked with age you'd swear she'd already croaked and been dug up.'

'Indeed not. Still as lively a woman as you could ever hope to meet,' chuckled his father. 'And, as you say, without shame.'

'Well, who'd have thought?' marvelled Methuselah, coming round. 'I could tell she was older than you, of course, but I'd have never guessed she was older than bubbe Barakah. What's that make her today, anyway?' He tallied up a few scores with his fingers. 'Adam was nine hundred and thirty, wasn't he? He died a good half century ago.'

Enoch nodded. He had queried Loogie and Eve as to why they outwardly appeared so much younger than others half their age. *We partake of ambrosia,* they'd blurted in unison – *the food of the gods!* And they'd both burst out laughing.

'It boggles the mind. And that man she's with? What's his name?'

'Loogie.'

'Ugh. A nature boy, I'm sure. Not from around here. All spit and phlegm. His tribe?'

'I don't recall that he told me,' replied Enoch, dissembling.

'It doesn't matter. One look and you can tell he's heathen.'

'Perhaps. At any rate, they've known each other a long time.'

The stock inference to draw from this was not lost on Methuselah. He scoffed.

'Father, I hope I don't sound dismissive here, but that's what I don't get when it comes to our elders. Why live so long? After a few hundred years, there's nothing new under the sun to see or do. Why, past a certain age, even love becomes a chore and a bore. I'm sure you agree: a bore and a chore.'

'Oh, I don't know. Even at her age, Eve, I can assure you, is still a fit woman. And Loogie, her companion, every bit a man.'

What the dubious son understood by this and what the father knew were two different things.

'Regardless, the point I was trying to make earlier, Methusy, is that if I'd let you and your bumpkin chums stone them like you'd wanted, I'd have never learned our true story. These past few days, Eve and her companion have been happily teaching your mother and me everything they know. It has been truly enlightening. I'll be reconsidering some of our rites. We'll continue with our mandated worship of Yah, to keep Him happy, but I will be looking for worthy members of our tribal family to be recipients of a new spiritual teaching, one whose initiates will enjoy the privilege and pleasure of entering into intimate communion with the heart and soul of life and love's mystery.'

'Well, for the love of God, please don't induct me into that,' said Methuselah. 'I've got enough to do already, what with all the prayers and sacrifices to Yah we have to offer each week. It never ends. And you want to sign me up for another religious ritual on top of all that? No thank you! I'm sure it's tedious as all get out.'

Enoch arched his brows but wasn't surprised.

'You needn't worry. Mysteries such as I've learned aren't for everyone, I'm sure.'

XXXY

CARESSED BY A CAPRICIOUS breeze, the tall grass was stirring with an undulating softness as Loogie and Eve ambled among the slender stalks and pulled at the panicles. The couple was gratified. Given the rocky rises nearby and the proximity of the desert's sands to the west, their sacred knoll had as yet escaped being overtaken by the organised cultivation that had transformed the Eden they'd known from a sprawling paradise of plenty into a tenant-walled checkerboard of systematised productivity. Here, at least, they could remember what had once been and see it anew.

'Well, what do you know,' said Loogie. He pointed to something he'd glimpsed hidden in the grass. 'Can you believe it?'

The tree had long since fallen, but the stone totem still stood where Eve and 'El and Asherah had placed it so very long ago. Loogie walked up to it and laid his hand on the smooth, rounded top. He smiled with the memories it kindled.

'Come here, you…' Eve put her arms round his waist and drew him close. 'Lie down with me.'

Stretching themselves out, they flattened some grass to create a secluded haven in which to snuggle. Loogie ran his fingers through Eve's long hair, softly combing the grey strands and contemplating her face. There was a pattern of creases etched by harsh treks in faraway lands, and furrows carved by worry and sorrow. There were crow's feet and laughter lines; the beginnings of a double chin; above the corners of her mouth, the once fine hairs of faint moustache had thickened and darkened with the years. As ever, her eyes were twinkling with mischief and love. She was the beautiful woman who had shared her life with him, with whom he had learned wisdom, who had walked by his side, blessed his nights with warmth and drawn him ever closer with unfading desire. He loved her as he loved life itself: with passion, with respect, with wonder and tender affection.

'It's awful what they've done, isn't it?'

'Awful,' he agreed.

'But I feel Enoch will chart a new course for the people here. He learned so quickly.'

'Of course he did. He has his great-great-great-great-grandmother's keen intelligence. Like most everyone else we've initiated down through the years. The mysteries are thriving, Eve – a blazing beacon of hope, a light of redemption for those who follow Yah in his darkness.'

'But Yah… will *he* ever love?'

It was the question they'd put to Asherah and 'El, on the eve of their return to the celestial spheres.

'Remember what they told us, Eve. Some day, Yah will learn to love. Just not in our lifetimes.'

A day is coming when we'll follow Abel, thought Eve. Ambrosia did not make mortals immortal; it held decline in abeyance, and they were still quite fit, but they could not hold on to Life's torch forever. One day, Death would pry it from their hands.

'I miss them,' said Eve, somewhat wistfully.

Loogie was walking his fingers up her back.

'They may return. Until our day comes, we can always hope.'

He kissed her forehead. They were lying where they'd spent their last hours with the two gods, gathered round the warmth of a crackling campfire. Asherah and 'El had related the tale of their head-to-head with Yah earlier in the day. It hadn't gone well. Their son had objected to what he contended were baseless insinuations.

'Calumnies!' he'd cried. 'I tell you, I did no such thing. It was the Devil!'

'You're saying *the devil* made you do it?' asked 'El cheekily.

'I'm saying the Devil is Evil, with a capital D! Whereas I am God! I am blameless! Always! Who are you to accuse Me?'

'We told you already. We're your parents.'

'That too is outrageous nonsense! I have no father! I have no mother! I am the First and Foremost! I am the G in GENESIS. The G in GOOD. G stands for Me, GOD! There is no other!'

'El raised his brows at this, but saw no reason to disabuse his son of his error. Truth was unalterable; it needed no defence.

'G or no G, it was *you* who raped Eve, and we are here to tell you, Yah, that *violence* – be it rape, or slaughter, or enslavement, cruelty, or coercion, even a tongue-lashing, or indeed *any* kind of violence – has no place in Creation. You must expunge your penchant for violence, Yah. Please – we entreat you to love.'

Yah had stood there fuming. *This 'El, as he calls himself, is a damned cocky pest. Oh, I'll smite him good!* And smite him good he would – the minute he could. Regrettably, in the presence of these two naked strangers Yah had been startled to intuit that his ordinarily limitless powers of retribution were inexplicably disarmed. If he tried anything and failed, he would lose face something fierce. Yah dared not court a blow to his pride.

'You are wrong,' said Yah, opting for lordly aloofness. 'I am a loving god. I love plenty. In fact, I am Love itself. But I am The One And Only God Of Love. There is no other like Me, and the beings I have created in My Image must worship and serve Me as I see fit. For so help Me, I am a jealous god. Indeed, My Name is Jealous – a consuming fire, a whirlwind of raging anger – and I will utterly destroy all who do not love Me as I wish. All beings must love ME – and *only* Me – with all their heart and soul!'

Asherah regarded her son with gentle forbearance.

'But, Jealous – love doesn't work that way, sweetheart.'

The endearment did nothing to mollify Yah's ire. He snorted, adamant in his animus towards this woman who'd refused – and refused still! – to bow in submission. *Sweetheart yourself! If I'd met you that night instead of Eve, I'd have drilled My first rule into YOU as I drilled it into her. FEAR THE LORD YOUR GOD!*

ღ

'El stirred the fire with a stick to send a gaily whirling spray of sparks skyward into the night.

'Before he stormed off, I told him, *You've got love all wrong, Yah. It's not about others loving you. It's about* YOU *loving others*

– with all YOUR *heart, with all* YOUR *soul – freely and unstintingly, receiving nothing in return.* THAT, *Yah, is what it is to love – and above all, what it is to be a god. For that is how a true god truly* LOVES…'

'It's hard to fathom how he could be so clueless, when he has you for parents,' said Eve. 'Do you regret he's your son?'

'No,' sighed Asherah. 'We love all our children and hope for the best. So no, we don't regret that Yah is our son. But his conduct? The inhuman way he's treated you? Yes – *that* we regret.'

In a wavering, valedictory dance, small flicks of blue flame were licking at the last of the embers in the firepit.

'Ash, truly – do you think Yah will ever learn to love?' asked 'El, poking at the coals to send more sparks aloft.

'Oh, yes, I think so, my dear.' She added with a laugh, 'When he's no longer Jealous.' Putting her arms round 'El's waist, she nuzzled his neck. 'Some day, he'll embrace Love. He'll become a true God – a god who loves, a god like *you*. But only when he comes to know Love, and love Love, as Love *is*… truly.'

'I'm afraid it's going to take him forever,' said Loogie, laying his head on Eve's shoulder.

'Never underestimate love. It can take ages, but little by little, even the hardest of hearts come round and yield like children to love's gentle ways. Thus will it be with Yah – though you and Eve, I'm sorry to say, won't live to see the day.'

The goddess sighed. Her eyes glistened with sadness.

'But, you're right, Loogie. It will be a long while yet…'

O

'I REMEMBER HER TEARS...'

'So do I. But I can still hear her words, full of hope – *Even so, rest assured... One day... O blessed day! ... Earth will become – and at last truly* be – *a paradise for lovers from pole to pole.*'

'We both felt so close to them that night.'

'The stars came out – '

' – the moon rose – '

' – we spooned – '

Gods and mortals had curled and cuddled and fallen asleep, melded together as one. But come the early morning, with the sun cresting the horizon to cast its warmth across Eden anew, Loogie and Eve had woken to find themselves alone.

They lay there in their grassy love-nest gazing into each other's eyes, bright as ever with love and desire.

Asherah had said they would not live to see the day.

But did it matter? They were here in the present, face to face, entwined with each other. Here, at least for now, they were in a lovers' paradise all their own.

With a come-hither caress and a tongue-dancing kiss, Eve and Loogie began to make love.

∞

Loogie

BY THE SAME AUTHOR

Les Jeux sont Fate

Qü@ñ†μм

The pig who wished to be a horse *...and other tales*

Jesus versus YHWH

The Gospel of Jesus of Nazareth

A·B·C· EDITIONS
17840 • LA BRÉE • FRANCE
ABCEDITIONS.COM

REMERCIEMENTS À
M.A. • R.C. • E.G.

IMPRIMÉ AU ROYAUME-UNI,
AUX ÉTATS-UNIS ET DANS D'AUTRES PAYS

LOOGIE

ISBN 978-2-9584200-7-9
PRIX PUBLIC LORS DE LA PARUTION • 24,69
DÉPÔT LÉGAL • AVRIL 2025

www.ingramcontent.com/pod-product-compliance
Ingram Content Group UK Ltd.
Pitfield, Milton Keynes, MK11 3LW, UK
UKHW040032170925
462928UK00022B/94/J

9 782958 420079